Dreams of

Dragon Shifter Romance

Mac Flynn

All names, places, and events depicted in this book are fictional and products of the author's imagination.

No part of this publication may be reproduced, stored in a retrieval system, converted to another format, or transmitted in any form without explicit, written permission from the publisher of this work. For information regarding redistribution or to contact the author, write to the publisher at the following address.

Crescent Moon Studios, Inc.
P.O. Box 117
Riverside, WA 98849

Website: www.macflynn.com
Email: mac@macflynn.com

ISBN / EAN-13: 9781791814571

Copyright © 2018 by Mac Flynn

First Edition

CONTENTS

Chapter 1 1
Chapter 2 8
Chapter 3 15
Chapter 4 22
Chapter 5 29
Chapter 6 35
Chapter 7 39
Chapter 8 46
Chapter 9 54
Chapter 10 60
Chapter 11 69
Chapter 12 76
Chapter 13 82
Chapter 14 88
Chapter 15 96
Chapter 16 103
Chapter 17 110
Chapter 18 117
Chapter 19 123
Chapter 20 130
Chapter 21 139
Chapter 22 147

Chapter 23..154
Chapter 24..161
Chapter 25..168
Chapter 26..173
Chapter 27..180

Other series by Mac Flynn.............................184

DREAMS OF DRAGONS

CHAPTER 1

It was dark. And cramped. And generally just damn uncomfortable

I shifted and winced as a stack of quills poked me in the back. So much for this being a good hiding spot.

A clatter of feet made me freeze. They paused. There came the sound of soft breathing.

"Where'd she go?" a small voice asked.

"I don't know, but she's gotta be here somewhere."

Please don't open the door. I moved again and winced as I was again stabbed by the unrelenting quills. *Please open the door.*

"What are you children doing in here?" a harsh voice snapped.

"Run!"

There was the clatter of feet and then silence. A heavy pair of boots stalked over to my hiding spot. I held my breath.

The pair of doors flung open and a sharp face stared into mine. The face belonged to a man, the former adviser of the kingdom of Alexandria, to be precise. His eyes widened and he leapt back with a high-pitched scream I didn't realize a man was capable of making.

I tumbled onto the hard floor and found myself on my back. Around me were dozens of long, tall shelves filled with all the knowledge of the kingdom of Alexandria passed down and painstakingly cataloged for future generations.

Also, one of its quill cupboards had been my hiding spot in a lively game of hide-and-seek.

Renner, the former adviser to Xander, glared at me. In his arms were a half dozen scrolls. The older gentleman had ditched his flowing blue robe with green hems for a plain gray robe with white hems.

He raised himself to his full, skinny height and looked down his thin nose at me. "What are you doing in here?"

I sat up and winced as my back popped. "Would you believe I was improving my mind?"

"I would not."

I stood and stretched my aching legs. "I wouldn't believe it, either."

A noise in the hall outside the doorway made me glance in that direction and forced Renner to half-turn around. "She's trapped, Darda! You have to save her!" insisted the small voice from before.

"Yeah! A mean man has her!" the other voice agreed.

"Has who?" Darda asked them.

Darda appeared in the doorway, and on each hand hung a small child. One was a boy of seven and the other a girl of five.

The girl pointed at Renner. "He has her!"

The boy's gaze fell on me and his face lit up with a smile. "Miriam! We found you!"

I jerked my thumb at Renner. "Actually, he found me first, so he wins."

DREAMS OF DRAGONS

Renner looked aghast at me. "You were using the sacred library as a game room?"

"No, as a hiding spot," I corrected him.

Renner's face turned an unsightly shade of red. Darda noticed and leaned down so she was closer to the height of the children. "Run along now. I must speak with Miriam."

Their faces fell. "Do we have to?" the boy asked.

"I want to stay with Miriam!" the girl whimpered.

"I think the chef has some cookies for you in the kitchen," Darda tempted them.

They didn't need a second invitation. The pair dropped her hands so fast that I think they snapped against Darda's sides. They bolted down the hall and their clattering soon faded away.

Renner boiled over like a cauldron left too long over a bonfire. "You dare use the library for your foolishness? You who is lady of this magnificent kingdom and Maiden to the great Xander?"

"It had the best hiding spots," I countered.

Darda hurried up to my side and faced Renner. "I believe what Miriam is trying to say is she meant no disrespect."

He snorted. "I dare say she did not! What is this library but the favorite place of her predecessor, the beloved Lady Catherine? Why not besmirch her memory for the sake of frivolous fun?"

I frowned. "I didn't mean any disrespect, especially not to Xander's mom. I was just trying to have fun with some of the castle kids."

Renner sneered at me. "*Lady Catherine* was capable of entertaining the children through *reading* the books, not abusing them."

"Sir Renner, I believe that is quite enough," Darda scolded him.

Renner's sneer dropped a little before he pushed past me and over to the quill cabinet. He knelt down and muttered a few words of which I only caught a handful. ". . .a shadow of My Lady. . ."

Darda looped her arm through mine and marched me out of the library. The smooth cobble stones were mercilessly pounded by her feet as she shook her head. "The insolence of that man! As though his own actions did not lose him the position of adviser! I will inform Xander of this outrage immediately."

"It's okay."

She whipped her head to me and furrowed her brow. "But he insulted you, Miriam! How can you be so forgiving over his unkind words?"

I smiled back at her. "Because *I* don't think I'm as much a lady as Xander's mom. I mean-" we stopped in the hall and I gestured to the head of a statue in an alcove. The bust was of the beautiful Lady Cate decked out in a tiara and with a bright, gentle smile on her face. "-there's about a dozen of these busts around the place, and that's just by this one artist. That doesn't include the portraits, the life-size statues, and even a dinner plate featuring her face."

"And there is the fountain statue in one of the courtyards," she reminded me.

I snorted. "See? It's a tough act to follow."

"But you saved the world many times," she countered.

"Yeah, but it's really hard to be patted on the back when most people didn't even know there was world-wide peril," I pointed out.

Darda pursed her lips as she studied me. "*I* for one believe you are as much a lady as Lady Cate. Well-" her eyes flickered down to my comfortable attire of jeans and a t-shirt, "-that is, in actions, if not in dress and manners."

I snorted. "Thanks. That makes me feel better."

"Are you ill?" a voice spoke up. We glanced down the hall to see Xander approach us.

DREAMS OF DRAGONS

I rubbed my back. "No, but I could use a massage after hiding in that cabinet."

Xander stopped before us and blinked at me. "Hiding in a cabinet? What was the occasion?"

"A game of hide-and-seek where it was two against one," I told him.

A smile slipped onto his lips. "Did you win?"

I stretched my back and winced as the lower part popped. "Yes and no."

Xander chuckled as he set his hand on my lower back just below the ache. "A massage would do you well," he mused as he led me down the hall.

"Might I offer my services?" Darda spoke up.

Xander looked over his shoulder and winked at her. "I believe I will handle this duty, Darda."

She straightened and her face blushed. "Oh! Yes! Of course!"

I glanced up at his mischievous smile as he led me in the general direction of our bedroom. "You're supposed to *relax* tight muscles, not tighten them further."

He chuckled. "I promise you will be very relaxed afterward."

We stepped through an archway and I tripped over a change in the flooring. Xander caught me before I fell and I got a good look at the floor. The smooth cobblestones of the hall changed to long wood planks. I raised my head and my face fell.

We stood in the lobby of the Mallus Library. The caretaker himself, Crates, stood near the wide opening to the countless bookcases. His hands were clasped behind his back and his expression was as dark as the books that lay in darkness. The whole place was illuminated only by a few candles that hung on holders beside the bookcases.

I straightened and frowned. "Come on. We didn't even go through a door that time."

Crates took a step forward and pursed his lips. "I apologize for the rough entrance, but we have much to discuss."

"You mean the two missing gods?" I guessed. He gave a nod. "Are they really that much trouble? I mean, it's been three months since our last fight and the world hasn't ended."

"The world continues to hang in the balance, though I have watched you from afar and must congratulate you on your many amazing feats," he complimented us.

"We couldn't have done it last time without our friends," I pointed out.

The corners of his lips twitched upward. "Yes. Like nature attracts like nature, and around you have amassed a wealth of such special people. However-" his face fell as he looked from Xander to me., "-the final two gods have made themselves known to me, and I feel I must warn you about one of them."

"How do they 'make themselves known to you?'" I asked him.

He swept his hand over the countless books at his back. "The vast knowledge of this library, and the location of your own battles, has allowed me to ascertain the identities of the remaining gods. Though I am bound to keep most information from you, I can warn you that one of those ethereal creatures is by far the most dangerous of any that remained in your world."

Xander arched an eyebrow. "In what way?"

Crates shook his head. "I cannot give you any specifics other than to say this creature will test your bonds-and even your sanity-like no other. You must keep your faith in one another and hold tight to what you know is the truth."

My face fell. "That's it? That's your 'specifics?' I get better advice from a fortune cookie."

His unblinking eyes fell on me and I shivered as I felt a cold chill sink into me. "You will tested the worst of all,

Miriam, so I will give you further advice: keep the chime to yourself and do not give it over to anyone."

I arched an eyebrow. "Not even Xander?"

"*No one.*"

I held up my hands in front of me. "All right, no one. Is there anything else you can tell us about this unspeakable evil?"

"You will know all too soon." He raised his hand and snapped his fingers. Invisible hands pressed against our fronts and pushed us backward toward the archway at our backs. Our last view of the old caretaker was of him raising his hand in farewell to us. "Good luck, my friends. You will need all you can find."

We were pushed through the archway and the view of the library in front of us vanished like a card in the hand of a magician. I looked up at Xander and frowned. "This sounds like fun."

He pursed his lips and gave a nod. "Yes. We have our hardest fights before us."

A thought hit me and I threw up my arms. "Crates didn't even tell us where these last two gods were!"

A horn blew loud and clear through the castle. Xander stiffened and whipped his head around so he looked at the front of the building that faced the lake.

"What? What is it?" I asked him.

His eyebrows crashed down. "Trouble."

CHAPTER 2

"Trouble? What kind of trouble?" I asked him.

"We shall see," he mused as he took my hand and led us to one of the many balconies that overlooked the lake and the majestic city of Alexandria.

The metropolis was spread before us for miles, but the trouble came from just below us along the surface of Beriadan Lake. The harbor was always crowded with the lively sea trade, and on an average day every ship imaginable could be found moored along the docks or close by.

Today, however, was a day for a more unusual vessel. The sailing ship had three masts that pushed its long, smooth body quickly through the mouth of the harbor and into the body of the lake. Three-mast vessels weren't unusual, but it was unusual to see the ship manned by a crew of men that all sported gold-colored dragon wings. The flag at the highest mast sported red and yellow stripes.

DREAMS OF DRAGONS

I looked up at Xander's tense face as he studied the ship. "Do you recognize the flag?"

He shook his head. "I do not."

"And the dragons?"

"They are also a mystery to me, and evidently to those who manage the harbor, or those at the mouth of the lake would not be blowing the horn." His keen eyes scanned the strip of land and rocks that through which the overflow from the lake escaped via a wide river. The river finished its course at the ocean far to the west of the city.

"It is strange. . ." I heard him murmur.

"What's strange?" I asked him.

His gaze fell once more on the vessel as it made its way toward the castle docks. "The journey up the river often takes a full day, even when the winds are favorable, but there was no warning of this vessel until this moment."

I watched the ship sail like a ghost to within a hundred yards of the castle where it stopped. "It looks fast."

Movement caught my eye and I leaned over the railing to watch a procession of guards exit the castle and march down to the port. Spiros was at the head, and he stopped the long ranks on the longest of the castle docks. An away-boat pushed off from the vessel, and besides the two rowers there was a single dragon man aboard.

"Lord Xander!" a voice called. We turned in time to watch a guard hurry up to the archway that led onto the balcony. He was out of breath, but managed to stand tall and salute. "A strange vessel has been sighted-"

"I can see that, but why was there no earlier messages about such dragons piloting the ship?" Xander questioned him.

"The vessel arrived at the mouth of the river only two hours ago and made the entire two-day trip in that time."

Xander's eyes widened. "Two hours? How is that possible?"

The guard shook his head. "We cannot tell except to say that the dragons appeared to use their wings to fan the sails."

Xander spun around to face the ship. I grabbed his arm. "What's important about that? The sand dragons can do that in their races, and even you could do it."

He pursed his lips as he watched the away-boat land. "Many thousands of years ago the art was commonplace, but as the years passed and we dragons drifted away from breeding with humans we lost that ability to manipulate our wings, and thus the sails. Now only small vessels of one sail and two dragons may be pushed by such methods, but not a ship as large as this."

I leaned forward to catch his gaze and frowned. "So what you're saying is these guys are like those ancient dragons like the Sæ made you into?"

The lead dragon in the away-boat stepped onto the dock and paused. He was about twenty with long blond hair that was nearly white in color. He wore black shoes, a pair of loose trousers, and a buttoned coat that hid all but the high collar of a white shirt. Even the eyes of the dragon were of a golden hue, but the smile that appeared on his lips felt cold as he tilted his head back and looked up at us as we stood some two hundred feet above him.

Spiros's lips moved, but I couldn't hear what he said. The visitor apparently didn't care to hear them because he opened wide his dragon wings and leapt up. He flew like a bullet, with each pump of his wings giving him an easy fifty feet of altitude.

Spiros drew his sword and gave chase, along with half the company of guards. They were half as fast so that the golden dragon reached our balcony well ahead of his pursuers. Xander drew me back and unsheathed Bucephalus.

The dragon crossed his arm over his chest and gave us a deep bow. "My sincerest apologies, Lord Xander, for the abrupt appearance of my vessel, but I bring an important message for you from my mistress."

Spiros and company arrived. The guards landed neatly on the railing, but the captain of them all dropped to the balcony beside our 'guest' and pointed the tip of his sword at the stranger. "An admirable flight, sir, but too short to escape us," Spiros informed him.

The man raised his head and chuckled. "If I had wanted to escape I would have merely flown to the tip of the castle and watched you weary yourselves in your pursuit. Therefore, it is fortunate for you and your men that I do not have any ill intentions toward your people."

"Your abrupt entrance would suggest otherwise," Spiros shot back.

A crooked smile slipped onto his lips. "If my men and I had wished to assault your castle than we would have hurried up the river. As it is, we merely moved as fast as the downstream current."

"Who is your mistress?" Xander asked the dragon.

The golden dragon swept his eyes over all the swords that were pointed at him. "It is of a most private matter, if you understand me."

Xander pursed his lips, but glanced at his old friend. "Spiros." The captain's eyes flickered to his lord. "Tell your men to stand-down, at least for the time being."

Spiros pursed his lips, but lowered his weapon and looked to his men. He gave a nod. The guards sheathed their weapons and took a step back. They dropped out of sight. I craned my neck and watched them glide down to the ground.

Spiros walked backward until he stood on the other side of Xander. Neither of the friends put away their swords. "If you do not mind, My Lord, I would like to stay."

Xander smiled at him. "I would like nothing better." He returned his attention to our 'guest' and his face hardened. "Who are you, and what message do you bring for me?"

The dragon bowed his head. "My apologies for not introducing myself at the first. I am Abraxas, and the vessel below us is my ship, the Acheron."

Xander started back. "Acheron? How did your vessel come to have that name?"

The man chuckled. "I am glad to hear there are still some in this world who remember the Acheron and the exploits of my crew."

I raised a hand. "Somebody mind filling me in on this mystery?"

Spiros pursed his lips as he studied our 'guest' with more consideration. "The Acheron is a ship of legend that disappeared some five thousand years ago. The ship was rumored to be crewed by the eldest sons of the highest houses, those that still retained a pure blood from the last of the ancient dragons. She was deemed lost at sea."

Abraxas chuckled. "She was not lost, but found, and by such a worthy mistress that she has no equal."

Xander frowned. "If what you tell us is true then how came you to live so long? Or are you a descendant of that ancient crew?"

Our 'guest' shook his head. "I am no descendant, but the dragon himself, as are my crew. Our mistress has granted us with eternal life so long as we stay in her service."

Spiros scoffed. "I would call that servitude, and your mistress a poor master."

Abraxas bowed his head. "We each serve our masters, though in different ways."

"And what message does your mistress wish you to relay to me?" Xander asked him.

"She wishes for an audience with you on her island," Abraxas informed him.

"Where does she reside?"

DREAMS OF DRAGONS

The captain smiled and shook his head. "That I cannot tell. I may only lead you to her, if you wish to accept her invitation."

"If she wishes to grant me eternal life than I am afraid I must decline," Xander told him.

"I am limited by what I am allowed to convey, but I can tell you that what she has to say is in regards to your hunting of her kind," Abraxas revealed.

"This woman sounds like she likes secrets as much as Crates. . ." I mumbled.

Xander arched an eyebrow. "'Her kind?'"

"Yes. She is a goddess."

I started back, but the men merely tightened their lips and their grips on their weapons. Spiros took a step in front of Xander and narrowed his eyes at our doubly-unwelcome 'guest.' "Does she mean to avenge her banished brethren?"

Abraxas shook his head. "Nothing of the sort. She wishes to speak with you about your hunting her, as she is well aware that there are few left of her kind in this world."

"She seeks a truce," Xander stated rather than asked.

Abraxas closed his eyes and bowed his head. "Of a sorts, but all that must be spoke of with my mistress. I am merely the messenger."

Spiros's eyes flickered over his shoulder to Xander. "Our foe wishes for us to stumble into her territory."

I snorted. "It wouldn't be the first time. Heck, it happened the last two times."

Xander relaxed his stance, but kept his sword at his side. "I must confer with my friends before I make any decisions."

Abraxas bowed his head. "As you wish, though I must return within the week to inform my mistress of your answer."

"So she's not the goddess of seeing-everything?" I guessed.

He chuckled. "No, and now that I believe I have said everything that I am able I must take my leave. If you wish to communicate with me I will gladly welcome you aboard my vessel." He bowed low to us before he turned and leapt onto the railing. The dragon spread his shimmering wings and launched himself far into the air. Xander, Spiros and I strode over to the railing and watched him sail down to the away-boat.

Today was turning out to be a hell of a week.

DREAMS OF DRAGONS

CHAPTER 3

The away-boat launched, taking with it the three golden dragons back to their perfectly pristine ship.

"For a mythical dragon he sure is scared of flying over water," I commented. I glanced across Xander and at Spiros. "So what was this guy and his crew supposed to be able to do that made them so famous? Other than disappear, that is."

"They were the first ship to explore much of the seas around the continent, as well as the first to discover the Island of Red Fire," he told me. "On their adventures they were said to have overcome the hardships on the Wild Isles and the first to break through the thick ice of the far northeastern shores."

"So exactly how dangerous would this crew full of ancient blue-bloods be to us?" I asked him.

"Among we dragons, only Xander would stand a chance against them," Spiros told me as he glanced at our dragon lord, "-but even he would find it difficult to tackle so many at one time."

"So we're screwed?" I guessed.

"If that phrase refers to our imminent defeat, then yes, we are 'screwed.'"

"And for that reason we will avoid conflict at all costs," Xander spoke up as he turned to us. His lips were pursed and his eyes uncertain. "I must accept the invitation."

Spiros frowned. "That could mean a trap."

"I expect that, and therefore will remain on my guard at all times," he promised.

"On *our* guard," I corrected him.

"On *all* our guards," Spiros insisted.

A hint of a smile slipped onto Xander's lips. "Do you expect to accompany me against my wishes, captain?"

"I expect to accompany you against the wishes of even a goddess," Spiros quipped.

"And I'm accompanying you because there's no way in hell I'm letting you get into this trouble alone," I added.

Xander chuckled. "I would have nothing less than my old friend and my Maiden by my side."

Someone cleared their voice behind Spiros and me. We turned and Xander looked beyond us. "Darda stood beneath the archway, and in her hands was the box that held the Theos Chime. "I expect you will be needing this, My Lord, along with my services."

"Could we keep you away?" I teased.

"No."

I shrugged. "Then I guess we're going to have to take you, though if this keeps up we're going to need a bigger boat."

"We will not accompany Captain Abraxas and his men aboard their own vessel, but rather charter our own," Xander assured me.

I cast him a sly grin. "Captain Magnus?"

"If he can be found."

DREAMS OF DRAGONS

"And if he can't?"

"Then he will be found."

Spiros stepped into our little conversation and smiled at each of us in turn. "Might I also suggest a priest to knock our 'friends' flat if they were to become rude, and to purify them if they were to become unruly?"

I blinked at him. "Who?"

"Apuleius. He is due to arrive within the day for a sermon at one of the local churches."

Xander nodded. "He will be a welcome addition as a matter of a healer."

I crossed my arms and frowned at the pair. "This is sounding more and more like we're storming a castle."

"I concur," Darda spoke up as she strode over to us. She turned to Xander. "Are we to expect such a fight?"

Xander glanced over his shoulder at the harbor and the golden ship below us. "I hope not, but hope is not what I would rely on for a meeting such as this."

"So does anybody know where Captain Magnus is?" I asked the company.

"Sailing the coast somewhere between here and Bruin Bay, but I will send my brightest and fastest crows to fetch him," Spiros promised.

Xander gave a nod at him. "Prepare them at once." Spiros nodded before he took to the skies to the highest peak of the castle where the crows roosted. My dragon lord turned to Darda. "Has the inscription on the chime changed?"

Darda shook her head. "I do not know, but-" she held out the box to him, "-we may find out."

Xander opened the box and drew out the major source of our victories over the gods, the Theos Chime. He tilted the bell back and studied the interior edge. A frown slipped onto his lips. "We may need Tillit. I cannot read this inscription."

I slipped up to his side and perused the words. "Why can't you read it?"

He glanced at me and arched an eyebrow. "You are able to read the inscription?"

I shrugged. "Yeah. It's there in plain English."

He shook his head. "Not to my eyes. How does the rhyme read?"

I cleared my throat and read the new rhyme:

Always behind, always in mind, to future is blind, to this you must find

Xander arched an eyebrow. "A strange rhyme."

I wrinkled my nose. "And how come only I can read it?"

"It may infer that you hold the most important part in what is to come," he mused.

I set the bell back into its box that Darda held. "If that's true than I'd rather be the only one *not* able to read it."

Darda tucked the box under one arm and looped her other arm through one of mine. "Reading it or not, we must prepare food for the journey." She glanced at Xander. "For how long do we expect this voyage to last?"

"Fill Magnus's cargo hold with food," Xander instructed her.

Darda gave a tug. "Then we had better begin the preparations."

"Why 'we?'" I asked her as she pulled me toward the arch.

"You thought yourself unfit for your position, so we shall fit you to the role of Lady of Alexandria," she reminded me.

I cringed. "I take it back-" my eyes flickered down to the box. I snatched it from her, "-and I'll take this."

Darda stopped and frowned at me. "Do you not trust me to carry the chime?"

DREAMS OF DRAGONS

"I trust what Crates the Librarian told me, and he told me to hold onto it myself," I told her.

She pursed her lips. "But how do you intend to carry the chime without a dress in which to hide it?"

I created a backpack with my water abilities and slipped the bell into the large pocket. "Easy, and I even have a few dragons in there in case someone might decide to get curious."

Darda sighed, but continued dragging me down the hall. "I will trust his words, but I do not like them."

My eyes flickered down to the box. It felt so light, but it held the fate of two worlds within its velvet confines. I sighed. "Ditto..."

Darda and I made the food arrangements in the castle's kitchen, a large room with a stone floor located on the bottom floor and at the back of the castle. The room was a steamy mess of delicious smells and burly women who might have been truck drivers in another life.

The burliest of them all was the head cook, a busty woman with an appearance of forty who waved a wood spoon at Darda like she wanted to bludgeon the handmaid to death with it. "What you ask for is impossible! I do not have that much food in the pantry and larders combined!"

"Then you might order some from the city," Darda insisted.

The cook shook her head. "I have just put in the order and sent it on its way! If you are not leaving today then I will not send another this day!"

"We will be leaving within the week," Darda told her.

"Then talk to me in six days! Until then you and your handmaid-" she pointed the offensive spoon at me, "-can leave!"

Darda frowned. "That is not my handmaid. She is the Lady of Alexandria."

The cook looked me over and scoffed. "Such a tiny thing? She has less muscle than my daughter-" she pointed at a burly young woman of thirty who hefted a fifty pound hunk of meat onto a butchering block, "-and she is small for her age."

I leaned close to Darda and lowered my voice to a whisper. "I'm guessing they don't eat what they serve us."

"She *is* the Lady of Alexandria, and the lord himself has commanded this food be prepared," Darda persisted.

The cook's eyes lit up at the mention of Xander. "Lord Xander? Why did you not tell me earlier and waste my time with your foolish requests?"

"Because My Lady-" Darda nudged me in the arm, "-wished for the task to be performed as well. Is that not so, Lady Miriam?"

I nodded like a bobblehead doll. "Yep. I wanted it done, too."

The cook sneered at me before she turned away. "I will have the food for you tomorrow. Anything that will keep in a hold will be ready, now leave! We must prepare!"

I stuck my tongue out at her as Darda pulled me away before we were bludgeoned to death by a wooden spoon. She guided me out the exterior door that led out to a narrow path along the side of the castle. The path wound its way along the high walls of the keep and down to the front gates.

She spun me around to face her so quickly that I learned what a spin-top felt like. "You must grow more confident in your duties!"

I frowned at her. "My duties?" I gestured to the door behind me. "I don't remember a list of lady's duties that included dealing with a caged rhino who only did tricks for the lord."

Darda grasped my shoulders. Her face was long as she looked into my eyes. "You are one of the most powerful beings in both our worlds, and yet you shy away from these duties as though they are a foe greater than yourself."

I turned my face to the side and sighed. "Maybe it's because I don't want to fail Xander, or you, or anybody else, okay?" A bitter smile slipped onto my lips as I returned my gaze to hers. "If I don't try then I won't fail, right?"

She sighed and her hands dropped from my shoulders. "Miriam, you have faced countless other adventures and trials with us, and have always prevailed."

I shrugged. "Yeah, but you guys are the ones that count."

Darda took a few steps forward so she stood even with me, but faced in the direction behind me. She looked into my eyes and a small smile slipped onto her lips. "There is no way we could ever believe you are a failure. Always remember that." She walked down the trail and around one of the winding corners.

I ran a hand through my hair and tilted my head back. A murder of crows flew over the castle in a northerly direction. They were Spiros's crows, gone to fetch Magnus so he could join us on another adventure.

"Another adventure. . ." I whispered. I closed my eyes and shook my head. "How do you get yourself into these things?"

CHAPTER 4

For the next two days a tense atmosphere hung over the castle. The presence of the Acheron didn't alleviate the concerns of my dragon lord as he stalked the halls and stood on the balconies awaiting a reply from the birds. The golden dragons never left their posts, but stayed in their positions like pale gargoyles.

On the third day I heard cawing. Darda was with me, and we both rushed out onto the nearest balcony and scanned the skies. I jabbed my finger at several black dots in the air. "There!"

The birds circled the air above the castle before they dropped onto a balcony above us. I leaned over the railing to try to catch a glimpse of the action, but to no avail.

Darda slipped her hands underneath my arms and opened her wings. My eyes widened as Darda leapt onto the railing with me in front of her. My feet dangled above a drop of some hundred feet.

DREAMS OF DRAGONS

I squirmed and whipped my head around to her. "What the hell are you doing?"

"Hold still, Miriam."

"Wait a-"

Darda stepped off the railing. I froze as stiff as a board as we dropped ten feet. She flapped her wings and caught a strong breeze off the lake that propelled us upward. My eyes caught a hint of movement beneath the waves.

Thank you I mouthed to my Uncle Beriadan.

Darda flew us to the upper balcony and we landed neatly on the hard floor. I stumbled out of her hold and into the strong arms of my dragon lord. I looked up and gave him a smile, but his attention lay on Spiros who stood nearby.

Most of the crows lined the railing, but one stood on Spiros's outstretched arm. In his other hand he held a small slip of paper. He read aloud its contents.

"Mathair shuigh could not hold me back. Will be there within three days."

A ghost of a smile slipped onto Xander's lips. "That is excellent news."

"Because we had no Plan B?" I guessed.

"Precisely."

"There are the warships," Spiros reminded him as he tucked the note into his pocket.

Xander shook his head. "That is not an option. If this goddess wishes only to speak with us than we must present as neutral a face as is possible."

Spiros snorted as he raised his arm and his crow flew into the air. The other birds joined their brethren and flew off to nest in the towers high up in the castle. "Captain Magnus's ship is hardly a peace vessel, as many other pirate ships and our own fleet can attest."

"We must hope that the goddess has not heard of Captain Magnus, and that the obvious age of the vessel and her tattered crew ill deceive her," he mused as he studied

Spiros. "Has Helle yet been able to guess which gods remain?"

Spiros pursed his lips before he shook his head. "Unfortunately, no. There were so many, and they left over such a long period, that she cannot even be sure how many of them there were at the beginning, much less who remains now."

"We are no worse off without that knowledge," Xander comforted him.

Spiros walked to the railing and looked over the side at the ship in the harbor. "Will you give them your reply this day?"

Xander shook his head. "No, not until Magnus has arrived. If he comes then we shall sail tomorrow."

Spiros turned to us and saluted. "Then I will prepare myself for the journey and inform Apuleius of our leaving." He strode off.

"Then I shall inform the kitchen to prepare for a heavy loading," Darda spoke up before her eyes fell on me. "Do you wish to join me?"

I winced. "I'd rather stay here for a bit. There's something I wanted to ask Xander, anyway."

Darda sighed, but bowed her head. "Very well. If you will excuse me." She left us alone.

Xander looked down at me with an arched eyebrow. "You have a question for me?"

I wrapped my arms around myself and looked down at the ground. "To be honest, it's less a question than a feeling."

"What sort of feeling?"

I shrugged. "I don't know. I just can't shake the feeling that something bad's going to happen."

"Have you heard the voices of the gods?" he wondered.

DREAMS OF DRAGONS

I snorted before I shook my head. "No. With so few left I think I'd be less worried if I could because then maybe I'd hear what this goddess was planning."

He took a step forward and wrapped his arms around me so that my side leaned against his chest. "You might remain here at the castle."

I whipped my head up to him and glared at my dragon lord. "Like hell I am. What would you do without my water powers?"

He chuckled. "Taking a shower would be made more difficult."

I rolled my eyes. "Great, I've been demoted to household plumbing."

Xander drew me closer and brushed his lips against my ear. "You will always be more than that to me."

I squirmed in his grasp. "Shouldn't we be thinking about other things? You know, like Magnus coming and our imminent deaths?"

He chuckled. "Magnus will arrive on the morrow and-" A loud horn sounded. It was the same one that blew when the Acheron arrived.

I dragged my hand down the front of my face. "Now what?"

Xander rushed to the railing and I reluctantly followed. We looked out over the lake and beheld two ships coming up fast from the river. The speed was so great that the sides of the vessels pushed huge swells onto the shore and its stern left bubbles in their path.

It was impossible not to recognize the fifty-foot long ship owned by the ex-pirate, Magnus Heinason that sailed in the lead of the other vessel. At the head of its bow sailed the majestic, half-naked mermaid. Even she looked like she had a surprised look on her face as the ship sailed up to the longest dock before the castle. The swells around the ship calmed and a shadow disappeared into the depths of the lake. The ship behind it was of the same design but with the name Rache painted on the side.

"Sailing upriver, fae style," I commented.

Xander glanced at me with a smile. "It appears your family has confidence in our ability to win."

I snorted. "Or my mom made Beriadan mad recently and he wants to help me kick the bucket."

Xander arched an eyebrow. "'Kick the bucket' means dead, correct?"

"Or a really painful way to injure a toe," I teased.

He turned to me and offered me his arm. "I will not allow either to happen, so let us greet our captain."

I snorted, but took his hand. "So you're going to start kicking all the buckets out of my-ah!" Xander swept me into his arms and pressed me away his warm, strong chest.

He smiled down at me. "If necessary, but hold on."

I looped my arms around his neck as he leapt onto the railing and into the sky. The warm lake breeze flew up and gently brushed against our skin as we flew in circles down to the castle port. The plank was just being lowered when we landed beside Spiros just feet from the dropped board.

Magnus stepped up to the top end of the plank and grinned at our little welcome committee. "A new record up the river, if Ah dare say it myself." He strode down the plank and grinned at us. "Only twelve hours. The bow hardly kept in the water."

"I am afraid you have not beaten the current time of two hours," Xander informed him.

Magnus frowned. "Two hours? What magic were they using?"

Xander nodded at the golden ship in the harbor. "The ancient magic of dragon strength."

Magnus followed his gaze and pursed his lips. "Ah, that vessel. Ah thought something was amiss with its crew of bright dragons. Ah haven't seen the like of it in my lifetime."

DREAMS OF DRAGONS

"Nor has anyone in many thousands of years. They proclaim to be remnants of the ancient bloods of Alexandria here on behalf of a goddess," Xander told him.

"Another one?" a voice mused. We looked to the plank and watched Tillit stride down the board. He stopped in front of us and shook his head. "I leave you for a few months and already you're in trouble."

"If you whine about it you can stay here with the rest of the children, *and* your cargo," Magnus scolded him.

Tillit wrinkled his piggish snout. "And leave you without Tillit's great knowledge of reading? You'd be lost without me."

Magnus arched an eyebrow as he studied the sus. "You can read?"

Tillit's face drooped along with his shoulders. "Et tu, captain?"

Xander turned his attention to Magnus. "I know Spiros's message mentioned the danger of this mission, but I want to reiterate the-"

Magnus held up his hand and shook his head. "Say no more, My Lord. If you need me and my crew then we'll take you to the ends of the earth, if that's what it takes. You'll be needing all the help you can get to manage a creature such as this. There's nothing worse in the world than a woman, and a goddess is double that." He noticed me and smiled before bowed his head. "Your person excepting, My Lady."

"And what about me?" a sharp voice spoke up. Alice, captain of the Rache and equal to Magnus in sea-strength, made her appearance at the top of the plank and glared down at her husband. "Without my help at the Straight of Obman this hunk of rotten wood would be a Mare fae's toy at the bottom of the sea."

I glanced at Tillit. "Where?"

"The Straight of Obman, or Deceit, is a nasty place in the north," Tillit told me. "The waters are so calm you can't tell the rocks under the water from the ones poking out. Lots of ships have gone down there."

"And this one would be among them if I hadn't been steering," Alice bragged as she marched down the plank and stood toe-to-toe with her captain. "So what were you saying about women and trouble?"

"Unfortunately, he is correct that the trouble before us may be twice as worse than any we have faced before," Xander spoke up.

"It's nothing a good ship and crew can't manage," Alice insisted. A sly smile slipped onto her lips as her eyes flickered to Magnus. "Which means I should go get the Rache and my crew."

Magnus puffed out his chest. "The Blå Engel is ship enough for My Lord."

"I would appreciate both ships. We may need as many hands as can be found," Xander told them.

Alice nodded. "Then it's settled. When do we leave?"

"As soon as you can be ready. We do not know how far we are to sail, so fill your holds with provisions," Xander instructed the pair.

Alice spread her wings and flew over to her ship that lay anchor a hundred yards from the dock. I watched her fly across the waters, and my gaze fell on the golden ship. Though the distance was far, I swear I beheld Abraxas on the deck looking back at us.

A cold chill ran through me, warning me that this adventure was going to be something else.

CHAPTER 5

A message was sent to Abraxas and our two ships were soon loaded. Their previous contents were deposited on the docks to be carried into the castle for safe storage.

Tillit patted the top of a large crate and sighed. "Farewell, furs. I had high hopes of selling you for a great many drachmas."

Darda glared at him. "Quit your melodrama. We will return and you will receive your money for your half-rate furs."

Tillit stuck out his chest and stood his full short height. "That's a cruel thing to say to me, my dear Darda. Tillit doesn't sell half-rate anything."

Darda scoffed. "I distinctly remember a certain pair of boots that were advertised as being made of the finest and strongest leather that inexplicably fell apart when My Lady walked through a puddle wearing them."

"That was faulty stitching, and in no way reflected the quality of the leather," Tillit argued.

"And there was another instance when a music box played the same note over and over and-"

Tillit cleared his throat. "Yes, well, mistakes can be made, particularly when so much product is moved over the lifetime of a sus."

"The 'sus' word being the most important," Darda quipped.

"Speaking of words," I spoke up as I took the chime box out of my backpack, "-I was wondering if you could read the rhyme on the bell."

Tillit smiled and bowed his head as I handed off the bell. "Tillit would be glad to do such a favor." He studied the interior edge of the bell and frowned. "I don't know this language."

Darda folded her arms across her chest and grinned at him. "I thought you could read *all* the languages of our world?"

"Tillit can, but this is gibberish," he insisted.

"Xander can't read it, either, but I can," I told him.

"What does it say?" he asked me.

"'Always behind, always in mind, to future is blind, to this you must find,'" I repeated.

Tillit studied the inscription a moment longer before he shook his head and handed me back the bell. "I still don't see it."

"I wish I could understand it," I mused as I stuffed the bell back into its box and into my backpack.

"Miriam, Tillit, Darda, the ships are prepared to leave," Xander called to us as he stood near the plank of Magnus's ship.

I adjusted my bag and smiled at the others. "Well, we're off on another adventure."

Darda sighed and shook her head. "May this one be as short as the winter days are long."

DREAMS OF DRAGONS

One of the sailors walked down the gangplank with a crate in his arms. On the side that faced us was a mark of eight dashes. One of his fellow crewmen grabbed his shoulder and jerked his head up the plank. "Not one of those. That one stays on board."

The sailor that lugged the crate wrinkled his nose. "But they smell."

"The captain's orders, now put it back." The sailor grumbled, but turned and walked back up the plank.

A smile slipped onto Tillit's lips as he stroked the stubble on his chin. "Very interesting."

"That box?" I guessed.

Tillit winked at me. "More like why the captain is keeping it aboard, but let's get up before they pull the plank out from beneath us."

We climbed aboard and the plank was pulled up after us. Magnus stood at the helm with his first mate, the vampiric Nimeni, by his side. "Open the sails!" he shouted.

The sails were opened and we sailed out into the open waters of the lake. The Rache sidled up on our starboard and we could see Alice at the wheel of her own ship. Magnus steered closer and nearly touched his sail posts to hers. Rather than blowing a kiss at her love, she raised a fist at him. He replied with a chuckle.

Xander walked to the port side railing and looked out on the Acheron. His lips were pursed as he studied the old vessel.

"I don't like that look on your face," I commented as I walked up to his side.

"Spiros's messenger crow returned with a message from our guide," he informed me as the golden ship opened her own sails. "He informed us that we would need to keep pace with them or be left behind."

I frowned. "Some hospitality. Do they also want us to paddle with our hands?"

"That might help if you have flippers," Spiros quipped as he came up on Xander's other side. His eyes flickered up to the sails that hung above us. "As it is, we'll have to hope the winds and currents are favorable to us."

The crew aboard the Acheron latched onto lines of rigging in front of the sails and opened wide their wings. They flapped their wings in unison, and from their appendages came forth blasts of air. The air filled the sails and pushed the ship forward at a speed that nearly matched a motor boat. The dragons flapped to the beat of a silent beat as they swiftly covered the surface of the lake and rushed down the river. They were also quickly outstripping our boats.

Xander spun around to face Magnus. "Can we not move faster?"

Magnus shook his head. "The wind isn't for us, My Lord!"

"If they remain at their speed we will lose sight of them in a few minutes," Spiros commented.

Movement in the water caught my attention. A greenish blue fish tail, larger than any fish in the lake, disappeared into the depths of the waters, but I could see their wake as they traveled ahead of us and down river. Twenty yards off the tail surfaced and slapped the water only to disappear again, but leaving their wake visible.

A sly smile slipped onto my lips. "So it's a game of tag, is it? You'd better be a better sport than Sala. . . " I muttered as I marched up to the bow and rolled up my sleeves. "And I hope this old tub can take this game."

"You've got an idea in your eyes that I don't think I'm going to like," Tillit spoke up as he came up to my side.

"If we can't push the sails then let's see if I can't push these ships," I told him.

"Is that wise to reveal your powers to these strange dragons?" Darda wondered.

DREAMS OF DRAGONS

Xander joined us at the bow. "The goddess approached us. That infers that she knows a great deal more than our names."

I stretched out my arms and clapped my hands together. The sound echoed over the roar of the river and off the trees that lined the shore. The water bubbled beneath our two ships and from the water ahead of the bows rose four large water dragons, two for each ship. They lifted their heads and released mighty roars that made the water ripple around us.

I leapt onto the bow of Magnus's ship and wrapped one arm around the neck of the naked maiden. "All right, boys-" I pointed a finger at the wake, "-after that uncle!"

The dragons dove their heads below the surface and took off across the water. They cleared the lake in a few seconds and dove into the river. The water was shallower so that the dragons were forced to raise their heads and some of their body. The crews yelped and clung to their positions as the ships rose a few yards out of the water. The ascension revealed vast colonies of algae and barnacles below the water line of Magnus's ship, though the Rache was clean of such intrusive creatures.

Alice glanced from the bottom of his boat to him. He sheepishly grinned at her. She rolled her eyes and shook her head as she resumed looking forward, though that wasn't necessary. I had the situation completely under control.

That is, until we started to catch up to the Acheron. The river wasn't wide enough for three ships, and they held the centerline position so that not even one could safely pass them on any side. I pulled up the invisible reins on my beasts and stopped the ships a few feet short of the collision.

Xander leaned out over the bow and squinted his eyes at the Acheron. I followed his gaze and noticed that the nose of one of my dragons was close to the stern of the vessel. My beast leaned forward a little too far and-for a millisecond-

I swore there was a distortion where the nose of the dragon caused a ripple in the rear of the Acheron.

Then the moment passed and the Acheron drew away from us. I let them create a gap of fifty yards before I matched their speed. A splash beside our ship made me look down to my left.

My uncle Beriadan swam beside us. His narrowed eyes lay on the Acheron for a moment before he looked up at me. "Fare well, niece, and do not trust anything that does not have a shadow."

I blinked at him. "A shadow?"

He raised his hand in farewell and dove beneath the surface, leaving me with a worse uneasy feeling than I had before. A tap on my shoulder made me look to my right where Tillit stood.

"We have trouble coming," he mused as he nodded in the direction of the stern.

I followed his gaze and cringed as I watched Magnus march his way over to us. "Begging yer pardon, My Lady, but give me back control of my ship!"

"It is the only way to keep pace with the other ship," Xander pointed out.

"Ah don't care if it's the only way to avoid the infernals! Ah want something back of my wheel!" Magnus insisted.

A faint noise caused us all to look across the gap between our ship and the Rache. Alice stood at the railing with a red face and her hands cupped over her mouth. "Get these damn dragons out from under my ship!" she shouted. I pointed at my ears and shook my head. "Get these damn things away!" I repeated my action and shrugged.

A sly smile slipped onto Magnus's lips as his eyes flickered to me. "On second thought, keep 'em." He gave me a lazy salute and returned to the helm.

I rolled my eyes. What a host of friends I had.

CHAPTER 6

We kept pace with the Acheron and near sunset the horizon of earth parted and the endless sea stretched out before us. Our guiding vessel slowed so that Magnus called out to me from the helm.

"That'll be enough, My Lady. Ah'll be taking control of my own ship again."

I plopped down on a nearby crate and my dragons that swam beneath us disappeared into the vast ocean. My mind ached more than my body. It took a lot of focus to keep those dragons intact, and my modern mind was hard up to the task.

Tillit took a seat beside me and smiled at my strained face. "You're getting stronger," he mused.

I wiped my brow with my sleeve before I shrugged. "My dragons did most of the work."

He shook his head. "It must take a lot of concentration to hold those beasts."

I snorted. "I'm just stubborn."

"You give yourself too little credit," Darda scolded me as she knelt by my side. She held a woven rope basket, and inside was a bountiful harvest of fruits, nuts, and a fluffy loaf of sliced bread. Darda held out a slice for me. "And you give too little thought to yourself."

I took the bread and bit a chunk out of it. "You two worry too much."

Darda looked ahead of us and nodded in that direction. "He, too, worries for you."

I followed her gaze and saw it lay on Xander. He stood near the bow with his back to us, but his head was turned just enough that I caught one eye looking at me. I gobbled down the rest of my slice of bread and walked over to him.

"Nice view," I commented as I leaned on the railing beside him. The setting sun glistened across the vast water. He continued to study me with his sharp gaze, so much so that I leaned back and frowned at him. "What?"

He pursed his lips and looked ahead of us. "I was wondering if you ever regretted my bringing you to this world."

I snorted. "You bringing me here? Believe me, the guy who brought me into this world was a heck of a lot uglier than you."

His tense expression didn't subside. "You were brought to this world on my command."

I arched an eyebrow. "Specifically your command?"

Xander nodded. "Yes. As the leader of the dragon lords it was my duty to execute the order."

I bowed my head and pursed my lips. "I see. . ." My befuddled brain couldn't think of a better response.

Darda came up behind me and set her hands on my shoulders. "You should eat more, Miriam, to keep up your strength."

DREAMS OF DRAGONS

Spiros joined Xander on his other side and clapped him on the back. "You have not touched a morsel, either, My Lord, and my instinct is telling me that our friends there-" he nodded at the white ship ahead of us, "-will demand we be at our full strength."

We ate and drank, but weren't merry. The supper was a somber affair as all our thoughts lay on the adventure ahead of us. Near the end Tillit raised his head to look at the stars that popped up overhead.

He wrinkled his piggish nose. "Aren't we heading a little north?"

Spiros nodded. "Yes, and westward."

"A little too much of both for me," Magnus spoke up as he joined our group. His lips were pursed as he studied the twinkling stars. "Ah'll be damned if Ah don't like a good wind at my back, but if we don't change course before midday tomorrow Ah'll curse its help."

I arched an eyebrow. "Why?"

He nodded at the dark expanse before us. "Because we're headed straight for the Ikuinen Myrsky."

I blinked a few times before I glanced at Darda. She leaned toward me and lowered her voice to a whisper. "The Eternal Storm."

I winced as I recalled those terrible winds and waves. "So they're what? Trying to convince us they're peaceful by tearing us to pieces?"

He shook his head. "Ah don't know, My Lady, but we'll know by midday."

The food was delicious, but the conversation left a bitter taste in my mouth as Xander and I retired to the captain's quarters under the wheel deck. The air was tense as we slipped into our night clothes. Well, I changed clothes with my water abilities and he slipped into nightclothes.

The bed was large enough that we could have taken our sides and been done. Xander gave me plenty of space as he took the wall side and turned over to face away from me.

I slipped beneath the covers and snuggled up against his back where I wrapped my arms around him. He stiffened.

"Relax," I whispered. He didn't relax. A snort escaped my lips. "You know, this reminds of my first date."

He tilted his head back so that one of his eyes rested on me. "You have had others besides me?"

I raised my head and a mischievous smile slipped onto my lips. "You weren't exactly my first." He frowned. I couldn't help but laugh. "Don't give me that face. You hadn't signed the order for my capture yet." His face fell. I wrapped a few water tendrils around him and gave him a good shake. "Don't give me that face. Anyway, as I was saying, this reminds me of my first date. The poor guy was shaking like a leaf, and when he tried to kiss me he closed his eyes too soon and ended up making out with a lamppost."

He arched an eyebrow. "That is an amusing story, but I fail to see how it relates to our current predicament."

I lay my cheek against his back and smiled. "Because if I close my heart to you you're going to keep being as stiff as that lamppost, and I mess up enough without kissing a lamppost."

I retracted my water arms as Xander rolled over and wrapped his strong arms around me. "No matter how you 'mess up,' you are perfect to me."

I snorted. "Don't tell me that. I already have these epic water powers, I don't need to have an inflatable head, too."

Xander chuckled as he held me close. Soon his even breathing heralded his ease into slumber.

Even with our reconciliation, my damned brain still wouldn't stop with the 'what-ifs' of my past. What if Xander *hadn't* given that order? What if I was still a normal human in a human world? Would I have been happier there than I was here?

It was a long time before sweet sleep finally took me.

CHAPTER 7

"All hands on deck!"

The loud voice jerked me awake. I stretched out my hand to sit up, but my palm slipped on the side of the captain's bed and half my body followed suit. I dragged the covers down onto the floor with me so that in a second I was tangled on the floorboards. Being so close to the unbending beams of the ship, I could feel the harsh rocking as swells shoved the ship from side-to-side.

The door to the cabin flung open. I looked up and breathed a sigh of relief when I saw it was Darda. "I thought you were a pirate," I told her as I tried to unravel myself from the sheets.

Darda hurried over and knelt beside me. "Now is not the time for playing in sheets, Miriam. The captain has called everyone to deck, and that includes you."

"Have we hit an iceberg?" I quipped as she drew the covers off me.

Darda tossed the sheets on the bed as I climbed to my feet. "No, it is much worse than that. We are coming upon the Eternal Storm."

I arched an eyebrow as I slipped into more appropriate clothing. "So soon?"

She wrapped her arms around one of mine and guided me to the door. "It is nearly noon."

I blinked at her as she opened the entrance. "Noon? Seriously?"

"Most certainly. You were exhausted, and Xander allowed you to sleep," she told me as we walked out into the bright light of day.

I blinked against the harsh brilliance, but the light was short-lived. Before us the Eternal Storm stretched across the sky, engulfing the sun in its terrible, rolling black clouds. Lightning jumped from cloud to cloud, and its thunder echoed across the sea. Boulders and jagged stones peeked out of the rough seas, inviting doom to whomever came close to their unforgiving shores. The wind tore at my clothes and slapped my hair into my face.

I brushed aside my unruly strands and looked out the bow. The white ship that lay ahead of us was aimed for the center of that maelstrom. Its sails were full open and all the pale dragons were at their positions undaunted by the rough waters.

Tillit slipped beside Darda and me as the ship rocked from side-to-side. "A good time to wake up. We're just about to enter our eternal sleep."

Darda glared at him. "The Storm has been escaped before and shall be again." I didn't have her confidence as I locked my legs to keep from falling over.

"Not if we're neck-deep in that mess-" Tillit nodded at the storm clouds and white waves, "-and if we're in that deep than we're over our heads in water."

Xander and Spiros stood at the back of the wheel deck with their hands grasping the railing. Magnus himself manned the helm. The grizzled old captain's face was pale as we approached the stormy seas. "Those bastards mean to beach us on those rocks, or drown us in those waves."

"Can the ship weather the storm?" Xander asked him.

Magnus shook his head. "Ah can't say for certain, but Ah know that no ship made of wood can win against those rocks."

Across a short distance of water stood Alice at the railing. She faced us and waved her hands above her head. That caught the attention of the three men and my small group. When she saw she had our focus she pointed at the storm and shook her head.

Magnus waved her off. "Bah! Stay behind if ya want."

Alice balled her hands into fists at her side and glared at her husband. She glanced at the helm and mouthed a few words. Tillit stood beside me and he started back.

"That crazy dragon!" he shouted before he whipped his head to Magnus. "She's coming aboard, captain!"

Magnus's mouth dropped open. "In this wind? That damned fool!"

Alice leapt onto the railing and spread her dragon wings out behind her. She leapt off the banister and into the chasm of water between us. The Rache turned port-side, widening the gap between the two ships and leaving Alice with no choice but to fly toward us.

A rough gust flew by and slammed into her. One of her wings was given an updraft while the other was thrown downward so that she was flung to one side and disappeared beneath the view of our deck.

Darda and Tillit raced for the railing, as did many of the crew of the Rache. I clapped my hands together, loud and clear. A block of water rose up between our two ships like a giant freight elevator, and atop it lay Alice. She was soaking wet and one of her wings was bent at an odd angle.

The Rache had stopped its turn away from us as the crew looked anxiously over their captain. Alice lifted herself onto her arms and waved them away. The crew reluctantly drew their ship away from the Blå Engel and in the opposite direction of the storm.

I drew Alice onto the deck and my water slid back into the vast ocean. Tillit and Darda helped her lean her good shoulder against a nearby pile of crates. Magnus moved to hand the wheel over to Nimeni, but Alice whipped her head up and glared at the captain. "Stay at the helm, you worthless captain, or I'll shove you overboard myself!"

Magnus froze and a grin slipped onto his lips. "That's my girl." He spun around to face his first mate. "Nimeni, what in all the hells are you doing at the wheel? Shove aside!" Nimeni arched an eyebrow, but 'shoved aside' so the captain could resume his position.

I hurried over to Alice, but kept behind my friends as they inspected her wings. Tillit grabbed the bent one and gave it a little tug. Alice yelped.

Darda slapped his hand away. "What do you think you are doing, Mr. Tillit?"

Tillit nursed his injured hand and frowned at her. "Inspecting the patient, my dear Darda."

"Inspecting her into an early grave," she quipped as she lifted Alice into a higher seated position. She glanced back at the sus and her gaze fell on his bag. "Have you anything useful in there?"

"Only what'll save my tail from something worse than a bent wing," he told her.

She sneered at him. "Your tail is hardly worth brushing, much less saving."

"Can I help?" I spoke up.

Darda nodded. "Yes. I need some bandages from my bag and a splint for this wing."

"I'll fetch the splint," Tillit offered as he stood and tottered off to a stand-alone crate.

DREAMS OF DRAGONS

I raced to the captain's quarters just as the storm took a turn for the worse. The waves swelled and dashed over the railing, soaking the boards. I stumbled to the door and slipped inside. Darda's bag lay hidden beneath the bed in that room.

The rocking had slid it out a bit so that I needed to only kneel down and draw it to me. I rummaged through the contents, namely her spare clothes and the chime box, and found a smaller bag filled with dried herbs and bandages.

I had just grabbed the roll of bandages when the ship lurched violently to the starboard side. The bag and I, not being nailed down, tumbled into the right-hand wall. The rear paned window swung open and the ocean washed in, drowning the bed covers and myself in seawater. I sputtered before I climbed to my feet stumbled over to the window. The panes were quickly latched and I hurried over to the door which I flung open.

The scene on deck was chaos. The crates of supplies, once neatly stacked, had been tossed about like sacks of flour. They lay shattered and their contents strewn across the planks that groaned under the strain of the storm.

The ship was shoved again, but this time it tilted toward the port side. I was thrown off balance and my shoulder slammed into the side of the stairs that led up to the wheel deck. A shadow fell down beside me and I felt Xander's strong arms wrap around me. He covered me with his body as he looked out on the gale.

The ship now sailed through the Eternal Storm. The seas were as rough as a wild boar and the clouds overhead shouted louder over one another in an attempt to drown out the whole world. Wave after wave washed over the deck, spilling the whole of the ocean over us. Through the thick mist of spray I could see Darda and Tillit, and between them was the injured Alice.

"What's going on there?" Magnus shouted above the storm.

The sailor in the crow's nest pointed at the waters on the port side. "Kjempeblekksprut!"

I looked up at Xander who's lips were pursed tight. "The what?"

"It means-" The ship was thrown again to the port side, and from the depths of the sea arose a monstrous limb.

The tentacle was as black as the clouds and as thick as an ancient tree. Suckers as large as my head dotted the surface and gradually grew smaller as they reached the wet tip of the thing. The tentacle was slick with slime as it stretched itself nearly even with the shortest of the masts.

"To swords, men!" Magnus yelled. "Your lives depend on it!"

The crew came up from the belly of the ship and crawled down the slick masts like monkeys. They brandished the swords at their sides and leapt at the tentacle, some from high in the rigging. A half dozen men sliced the tendril, cutting deep into its soft flesh.

A great roar was heard that drilled into my head. I clapped my hands over my ears as some of the sailors stumbled back. The tentacle aimed its suckers at them and fired, shooting thick black balls of gunk at the men. The velocity shoved them to the deck and pinned them there in its unforgiving stickiness.

The ship was pushed to one side like a toy in a tub as a greater shadow rose up behind the tentacle. It was the bulbous body of a huge squid. The creature's black eyes stared unblinkingly at the trapped men. It opened its awning man, full of razor sharp teeth, and lunged at them. The men raised their hands and screamed as it descended upon them.

One moment their doom was certain, and the next Nimeni stood between the crew and death. He was without sword, but not without weapon. At his sides hung his hands, and his fingers were as long as knives and just as sharp. He leapt upward at the beast and they met at the railing. The vampire drew his hands forward and sliced with a speed I

DREAMS OF DRAGONS

couldn't follow. Cuts appeared on the slick face of the creature like black magic. It roared and reared back, dragging its tentacle with it.

Nimeni neatly landed atop the railing, bu turned and leapt down to the deck. He swiped his claws through the gunk, but the thick goo took several cuts before it would release even a single one of its victims.

"Remain here," Xander ordered me as he hurried to help with his own claws.

I clung to the side of the stairs and watched the pair free one sailor after another. The two of them worked away at the gunk while the storm worked away at the integrity of our ship. The beams creaked and groaned under our feet, and each rough wave dashed to pieces another piece of cargo on deck.

One of the groans sounds odd to me. I knelt down and pressed my hand against the water that coated the planks. My mom's old warning about touching the ocean echoed through my mind as I closed my eyes. Still, a little cheating wouldn't hurt.

It did.

CHAPTER 8

A sharp pain stung my brain as images flashed through my mind. The ocean's violent movements were like a heavy-metal song that vibrated my mind with its countless voices singing in different tunes. Schools of fish clamored for my attention above a strange whale-like creature. Sharks flitted to and fro around the edges of the storm, waiting for an easy meal provided by the rough seas.

Then there was the voices from land. Countless voices of people and animals that disturbed the ocean. Divers and fishermen plied their trade. Animals crossed the shallows in search of a place to rest, and their footsteps were like thunder to my mind.

A gave a shuddering gasp as I tried to focus my attention on the small area around us. The ship itself left a wake in the seas and my mind, though even the rough waves couldn't slow down the impressive speed of the Blå Engel.

DREAMS OF DRAGONS

She barreled through the ocean like an angry rhino intent on conquering the storm, or go down trying.

Something beneath the ship had that second option in mind. I jerked my hand back as my eyes flew open. I whipped my head to Xander who stood over a trapped sailor some forty feet from me. "There's three of those things!"

He paused in his saving and glanced over to me. "What?"

I cupped my hands over my mouth and took in a deep breath. "There's three of-"

The ship rocked violently to and fro as three large forms burst from the ocean around us. Two lay on our port side and one on our starboard. Magnus spun the wheel to and fro to keep us on course while also dodging the overgrown ink jets. Our former opponent lay off a few feet further than the others, and like a general he splashed his tentacle into the water as a sign to charge. The other two the creatures raised three of their tentacles above the deck and brought them down.

I dropped to my knees and flung up my arms. The water on deck shot up and knocked the tentacles back. The squids screeched and tried again, and again I parried them with my water magic.

As I dueled the pair our third opponent swam fifty yards ahead of our ship and stopped in our path. It stretched is tentacles wide to block any hope of preventing a collision. I threw a column of water ahead of us, but the other squid latched onto its lower half and sliced it through, breaking contact. The other half fell with a hard splash into the ocean.

Xander sprinted toward the bow, dodging the chaos of trapped men and ruined cargo. His wings burst from his back, but kept close against his body as the wind whipped at his person.

Darda tried to grab him as he passed them, but Tillit shoved her hand down. She glared at him. "What are you doing? His wings will be torn apart!"

Tillit grinned as he shook his head. "Not our dragon lord, my dear Darda."

Xander reached the bow and leapt into the air. He spread his wings wide and the wild wind filled them. As he flew onward his body transformed into the behemoth dragon of legends. His form rivaled that of the giant squid so that when they collided it was an even match. The pair slapped, bit, and clawed at one another in a fight to the death.

The squids around us tried to break away and join their comrade. "Where are you going?" I called to them as I raced across the slippery deck.

I reached the bow and hugged the back of the majestic mermaid, so akin to my cousins. The pair of squids were fifty feet ahead and gaining distance. I took a deep breath and threw up my arms.

From the depths of the turbulent seas arose four huge dragons. They blocked the path of the squids and lunged at the creatures. The squids scuttled back and threw their gunk at the dragons, but it was like hitting-well, water. The gunk was absorbed by the bodies of my dragons, but the squids couldn't say the same about the bites of my dragons. My pets clamped down on their heads and the pressure from their watery jaws allowed their wet teeth to sink into the soft skin of the creatures.

The squids screeched and dove beneath the water. My water dragons dove in after them and gave chase through the wild waves. The dragons nipped at the heels of the squids until the beasts swam off in separate directions and disappeared.

A weak screech turned my attention back to Xander. He leapt backward off his prey and revealed the squid in a sorry state. Its head was a mess of cuts and long gashes, courtesy of Xander's claws and fangs. The squid fell backward into the water, leaving a trail of black blood in the rocking ocean.

DREAMS OF DRAGONS

A smile slipped onto my lips as Xander roared over the pool of blood and turned back to the ship. My self-congratulations was short-lived, however, when a dizzy spell overtook me. My legs gave out beneath me and I fell to my knees onto the cold, unforgiving planks.

"Miriam!" I heard Darda shout. Her feet pounded across the deck and she was soon by my side. She grasped my shoulders and tilted my side against her chest. Her wide eyes swept over me. "What is it? Are you hurt?"

I gave her a weak smile and shook my head. "No, just my-" I winced as a pain shot through my head. It felt like someone had shoved a drill into my skull and given it a twist.

Xander-back to his human self plus wings-landed near us and joined us on my other side. His eyes gave a cursory study of me before he looked up at Darda. "What happened?"

She shook her head. "I do not know. She merely collapsed."

"I'm still awake," I reminded them as I tried to draw myself from Darda's hold. She held fast.

"You should not try to walk," she scolded me.

I frowned at her. "I wasn't going to walk, I was going to float on water back to the cabin, now let me up."

"Allow me," Xander spoke up.

He slipped his arms beneath me and lifted me against his chest. It was hard for me to argue against the feel of his firm, warm chest against my side. I snuggled close, but still glared up at him. "I can walk."

"And I look forward to watching you, but at another time," he teased as he strode across the deck with Darda following close.

The ship rocked to and fro, but without the homicidal seafood to bother us the vessel sailed straight and firm. Still, we weren't out of danger yet. Around us was an endless sea of storms, and we were fast approaching the rocks.

We reached the point on the deck where Tillit and Alice knelt when I grabbed the front of Xander's shirt and gave a tug. "You're forgetting the storm. Don't put your water weapon away until we're out of this wet mess."

Darda glanced over her shoulder and looked at the bow. "Where did the Acheron go?"

"Left us to sink to the bottom!" Alice spat out as she staggered to her feet. Tillit leapt up and let her lean on him as her furious face looked out over the ocean. "To sink in this wretched, foolish trap!"

"Captain!" the sailor in the crow's nest shouted. Everyone tilted their heads back to see that he pointed at the seas ahead and just to the left of our position. "I see a break in the storm!"

Magnus spun the wheel. "And Ah'll be damned if Ah don't take it!"

The ship turned at the bidding of her master and sailed through the choppy seas into the field of jagged rocks. Magnus's mastery of the helm was on full display as he turned the wheel to and fro to avoid the ship colliding with one of those widow-makers. His crew helped by drawing the rigging and setting the sails at each of his orders.

After a few tense minutes I could see what the eagle-eyed watchman had noticed. There was a break in the clouds that held a beautiful blue sky. The closer we came the more the rocks smoothed and flattened themselves. They connected and became larger masses of land like a small chain of islands islands. I squinted my eyes as we passed a particularly large island. I swore I saw some tumbled columns jutting out from the black stone. Then it was gone.

The ship broke through the storm, and it was like passing out of a waterfall. The rough seas died away and the rain slowed to a drizzle until only a few bits of spray hit us, and even that stopped.

Still, we weren't entirely safe. The area we entered was in the center of the storm, and the clouds that we just left surrounded us in a huge circle, daring us to enter its domain again. The rocks, too, were left behind, but with the bright light I could see they formed a chain around the clear area so that the only exit was the way we'd come inside.

A gentle breeze still blew, and it guided us like an arm toward the center of the calm. All of our attentions turned to that point.

Tillit climbed to his feet and gaped at the view. "By all the gods."

The phrase couldn't have been more appropriate. In the center of the perpetual storm arose an island of black rock. Atop that rock stood a large mansion in the style of an English palace. The building had four floors and stretched in a rectangular shape from our left to our right, and was half as deep. There was a flat roof atop which ran a parapet, and each of the four corners was punctuated by stone towers topped with cones that stabbed the sky. The outer wall was hewed from the dark rocks of the island and stood out against the blue sky like a gash. The windows were tall and narrow with paned glass to cover their insides.

In front of the palace was a small flat area. Once a row of columns had guided visitors to the front doors, but now they stood askew or were completely knocked down. At the end of the procession of columns was a large stone archway nearly perfectly intact, but weathered smooth by time.

A dirt road wound its way down from the archway to the edge of the island. A long dock jutted out from the rocks. On the left of the dock I saw the Acheron, parked and devoid of its crew.

Magnus guided our ship near the dock, but before we reached it he cupped one hand over his mouth. "Ease up on the sails, lads!" The sailors did as they were bidden and rolled the sails up to their beams. The ship slowed, but didn't stop. "Drop the anchor!" The heavy anchor was dropped and the ship dragged on for a few more yards before she came to a stop.

Magnus handed the command over to Nimeni and strode down the stairs near us. "Begging yer pardon, My Lord, but Ah don't like the look of this one bit. Seems to me like it was too easy getting here."

Darda scoffed. "Too easy? We were very nearly killed several times!"

Magnus nodded at the storm at our backs. "Ah've had my fair share of those storms, and each time its tried to batter me away. This time Ah almost felt like it was trying to drag us in."

Spiros arched an eyebrow. "So what you are suggesting is that a weakened storm that only harbored a slight inclination to destroy us is something to suspect?"

"What this fool is trying to say-" Alice spoke up as Tillit drew her closer to our circle, "-is that whatever we're dealing with is strong enough to be playing with a storm that's dashed apart more ships than there are in the entirety of all the fleets of the world."

Magnus nodded. "Aye, that's the rub. What sort of a creature is this 'god' of theirs that its calming something even Ah couldn't navigate."

A sly smile slipped onto Alice's lips. "Have you forgotten about that incident in my boudoir?"

The captain frowned. "Ya damn women and yer infernal dressing rooms are meant to trap men."

As some of our crowd smiled at their antics, Spiros turned to Xander and me. "What are your orders, My Lord?"

Xander pursed his lips as he looked down at me. "We will remain here for a time until Miriam has recovered, and then venture onto the island via one of the away-boats."

"I'm fine," I insisted.

DREAMS OF DRAGONS

"We'll let the ship's doctor decide that," Magnus told me.

I frowned. "Who's that?"

Magnus grinned as he glanced up at the wheel. "Nimeni, Ah've got a patient for ya!"

CHAPTER 9

"*A vampire?*" I hissed as Xander set me down on the bed in the captain's quarters. A mess of fluffy pillows lay under me, but they didn't provide me comfort as I frowned at my dragon lord. "He wants a *vampire* to look at me? What's he going to do, bleed me?"

"Nimeni has been on this earth far longer than any of us," he assured me as he took a seat on the side of the bed. "If there is anyone who might find a cause to your pain then he would be that man."

"*Vampire,*" I reminded him.

The cabin door opened and in stepped Nimeni, fresh from being relieved of the wheel by the homicidal captain. He shut the door behind himself and bowed to us. "I hope I am not intruding."

"Yes."

"No."

DREAMS OF DRAGONS

Nimeni arched an eyebrow. "Should I return at a later time?"

"Yes."

"No."

I glared at Xander. "I'm fine. My headache's gone and I-" I tried to swing my legs over the side of the bed, but a dizzy spell struck me. The world spun around me and I spun with it. It was only thanks to Xander's steady hands that I was laid back on the pillows. "Mostly gone."

His boots clacked hard against the floor as Nimeni strode over to us. He stopped near Xander and bowed his head to the dragon lord. "If I might have a word alone with your Maiden, My Lord."

I latched onto his hand faster than a kid on an ice cream cone. "Don't you dare!" I whispered.

Xander pursed his lips as he looked up at the vampire. "Is it necessary?"

"Absolutely."

Xander returned his attention to me and smiled as he stood, nearly taking me over the bed with him. "I will be just outside the door-"

"Don't leave me!" I insisted.

He stepped backward toward the door. "-and at your call I will-"

"Xander!"

"-come." Xander reached the door and slipped outside.

There was a click as the door latch fastened. Movement caught my eye. I whipped my head to Nimeni. The vampire had grabbed a chair and walked it over to the bed. He took a seat facing me with his unblinking eyes. They were red.

I scooted back until my side hit the wall. My sheets were a poor cover, but I drew them up to my chin. Nimeni sat as still as a statue and continued to stare at me. He didn't move an inch. There also wasn't any breathing activity in his chest.

I swallowed the lump in my throat. "W-well? Aren't you going to get doctoring me?"

"Do you wish me to?" he returned.

I snorted. "What do you think?"

"That you fear me. You are trembling."

I tried to stop my shaking and raised my chin up. "I-I'm just cold. It was all that sea water."

Those damn eyes of his didn't blink. "Is that what caused your headache, as well?"

I shrugged. "I don't know. You're the doc."

"Will you allow me to be your doctor?"

I pursed my lips as I studied that pale face and those red eyes. "Yeah. I mean, it's not like you haven't saved us a bunch of times." I sighed and scooted closer to the edge of the bed. "So where do we start?"

He stretched out his hand. "I need your hand."

"Why?"

"Because I need your blood."

My back returned to the wall. "M-my blood? For what?"

"To make an accurate diagnosis."

My eyes widened. "*That's how you tell if people are sick?*"

"Yes."

I shrank down and grimaced. "Is that the only way?"

"Yes."

My eyes flickered to the door. It was still shut, but a shadow moved under the door. I took a deep breath and inched my way over to Nimeni. The vampire hadn't budged an inch except to hold out his hand. He hadn't even blinked. I set my trembling hand atop his.

He leaned down and pressed his lips against the top of my hand in a soft kiss. A blush accented my cheeks at his gallantry, but it was short-lived. In a moment he flipped my arm over and I saw a flash of long, white teeth. They sank deep into the soft flesh of my wrist. I opened my mouth to cry out, but the pain was gone. So was Nimeni.

One moment the vampire sat in the chair and the next he stood in a corner across the room near the door. He clutched his chest over his heart with both hands and his eyes were wide. His body trembled like mine had and his face was contorted with pain.

"Nimeni?" I called to him. He shut his eyes and doubled over. I tossed aside the covers and stumbled over to him. "Nimeni!"

My voice brought Xander. He flung the door open and rushed over to me before my weak legs gave out. I pointed at Nimeni who was partially hidden by the entrance. "He needs help!"

Xander looked over his shoulder just as Magnus stalked into the cabin. "What's going on?"

Xander nodded at the shaking vampire. "Your first-mate is now ill."

Magnus turned and drew aside the door. He frowned as he looked over his mate. "Ya damn fool. Ah only wanted ya to take a look at her. Ya know you've never taken blood from a half-fae, much less someone as strong as My lady." Nimeni slipped to his knees and bent over. Magnus hurried to his side and gave his back a pat. "Easy there, Nim. Ya know ya shouldn't be fighting it."

The vampire raised his head and opened his eyes. They were no longer red, but a bright blue.

Magnus started back. "By all the gods. What has the blood done to ya, Nim?"

Nimeni shut his eyes and clenched his sharp, pointy teeth. When he spoke his voice rattled like an old fence in a rough wind. "The ocean. The vast sea. So-" he paused to turn his head to one side and shudder, "-so much. Too much."

Xander glanced at me. "Did you touch the ocean?"

I shrugged. "Sort of?"

He frowned. "Did your mother not warn you to avoid touching the ocean?"

I returned his frown with a glare. "I needed to do it to save the ship!"

"You should not have endangered yourself."

"It was worth it!"

"My Lord. My Lady," Magnus spoke up as he hefted one of Nimeni's arms over his shoulders. The vampire's head hung forward and his body was limp. "If ya don't mind, Ah might need to have my mate get some rest."

I turned to him and my face fell. "Is he going to be okay?"

Magnus looked down at his mate and grinned. "Aye, but he'll be needing a bit of time to recover. Yer blood was a bit much for him." He carried Nimeni so they stood beside us and paused to look me over. "But yer looking a might better, so Ah think he'll be happy for what he's done."

I glanced down at myself. My body had stopped shaking. I raised my finger that he'd bitten. The wound was gone. I looked up at Magnus with wide eyes. "He...Nimeni did that?"

He nodded. "Aye. Ah can't speak for yer old home, but a vampire's a powerful thing in this world. He healed ya right up by taking out the bad blood and sucking it into himself." He gave me a wink. "If ya don't mind my saying, he's probably honored to be biting such a pretty young woman. It ain't often he's got any more than the men to be healing."

Magnus left me with a lot of different, and slightly unpleasant, images as he dragged his mate over to the bed. Xander set his hand on my lower back and guided me over to the door. Our friends waited for us outside, and the clear light of the sun above us showed their concern.

DREAMS OF DRAGONS

Darda walked up to me and set her hands on my upper arms. She studied me with her sharp gaze. "How are you feeling?"

I smiled at her. "I'm just fine. I only touched some water I guess I shouldn't have."

Tillit arched an eyebrow. "More of that water sight?"

I nodded. "Yeah. I'll just be more careful next time."

Alice sat nearby on a mostly-intact crate. Her wings were folded behind her and the injured one was expertly wrapped in Darda's bandages. "What's this about sight?"

Tillit turned to her with a grin as he gestured to me. "Our lovely Maiden here has the ability to not only put a goddess's beauty to shame but to touch water and know what's happening in it countless distances away."

Alice studied me with a careful eye. "So you'd know when a ship was coming along the seas?"

I shook my head. "I can't touch the ocean. It's a little too much for my mind to handle."

Spiros's gaze fell on Xander. "What are your orders, My Lord?"

Xander lifted his eyes to the palace. Nothing stirred on that barren island save for a gentle breeze. Even that seemed empty as it had nothing to stroke but the few dead weeds that stood around the archway as though they were worn people bowing to the former majesty of the place.

"We will have an audience with this god, but the ship should be made to leave at a moment's notice should our meeting not go as planned."

Tillit snorted. "You mean as well as it's gone so far with these rascals." His eyes flickered to Spiros and he bowed his head. "Your wife notwithstanding."

Spiros shook his head. "I perfectly understand, and am quite glad to be rid of my rather troublesome in-laws."

Tillit strode up to Xander's side and looked up at the dragon lord's pensive expression. "When are we to go?"

"Now."

CHAPTER 10

An away-boat was ordered by Magnus and my many friends and I were stowed away in its interior. Tillit and Spiros received the oars while Xander sat at the bow. Darda and I took the stern with my hand on the rudder. Magnus and Alice stood on deck beside the boat.

The captain stepped up to Xander. "We'll be at the ready whenever ya come back, My Lord, even if we see ya flying."

Xander smiled and bowed his head. "And we will try to return your away-boat, if possible."

We were launched, and Spiros and Tillit took up their oars. The pudgy sus was hard-put to keep up with the ambitious dragon captain so that the ship was many times turning towards the rocks rather than the dock.

"A little more pushing, Master Tillit!" Spiros scolded his other half.

DREAMS OF DRAGONS

The sus huffed and glared at him. "A little less pushing, Captain Spiros."

Our unorthodox route to the dock gave me ample time to study the island. The house was half as deep as it was long, and many of the windows were shuttered like eyes shut out to the world. A light mist ghosted over the rugged terrain and floated down the hill like a cold reception party. The waves splashed against the rocks that surrounded the island and from their union came a haunting wind that made me shiver.

I wrapped my arms around myself and tried to wipe the goosebumps from my arms. Darda noticed. "Are you feeling well?"

I smiled and nodded. "Yeah, just a little cold."

"That's the taking," Tillit wheezed as he stroked for all his chubby life was worth.

I furrowed my brow at him. "The what?"

"That's-*gasp*-that's what happens when a vampire takes your blood," he explained. "They-*wheeze*-take a bit of your life to do it-*gasp*-so you feel colder."

I pursed my lips. "Any other side effects I should know about?"

Tillit paused in his rowing and wrinkled his piggish nose. "Well, there's-"

"Tillit!" Spiros scolded him as our boat began to turn in a circle.

Tillit put all his weight into his rowing and the boat was righted. The extra output of energy also glided us within jumping distance of the dock so that soon we slid into a berth opposite the Acheron. Xander tied the front rope to the dock and Darda took care of the back.

Tillit slumped over his oar and groaned. "Tillit is not made for this sort of work."

Spiros slapped him on the back and grinned. "You did well, my portly friend."

My dragon lord was the first to disembark from our craft. The boards creaked beneath his feet as he took a few steps down the dock. We all stiffened as a figure appeared down the road and onto the dock. It was Abraxas, and he was as quiet as the tomb as he made his was over to us.

"I am glad to see you survived the storm," he greeted us with a smile and open arms.

Xander didn't extend the greeting, but rather looked past Abraxas at the palace. "This is the residence of your mistress?"

Abraxas half-turned and his gaze fell on the large home. "Yes. She has maintained this home for quite a number of years.

As the rest of us climbed out Tillit nodded at the far-off island with its ruins. "Looks like your mistress forgot a spot."

"Unfortunately, it is a chore enough for her to maintain this residence, so that anything outside the confines of the house has fallen into disrepair, notwithstanding the dock," he explained before he swept his arm toward the home. "If you would follow me."

Abraxas led us down the dock to the dry, hard ground. Tillit paused and glanced over the side of the dock. His brow was furrowed and his lips tightly pursed. I followed his gaze and saw only our distorted reflections in the constantly shifting water.

Darda came up behind him and frowned. "We haven't time to waste on your dawdling, Mr. Tillit."

He shook himself and smiled at her. "There's always time to waste, my dear Darda," he told her as we moved along.

Xander walked shoulder-to-shoulder with our guide while Spiros followed close behind. The captain looked up at the swirling clouds that nearly blocked out the sun. "How is it your mistress has been able to reside inside such a storm?" he wondered.

DREAMS OF DRAGONS

A crooked smile slipped onto Abraxas's lips. "My mistress is the creator of the storm."

My friends and I stopped in our tracks. Xander frowned. "Is she the goddess of storms?"

Abraxas shook his head. "I am afraid I cannot tell you very much of my lady, only that she is eager to see you. If you would come this way."

We climbed the hilly road to the arch. I paused beneath that ruined edifice and half-turned back to look at the way we'd come. Where I stood was the highest point on the land and gave me a expansive view of the eye of the storm. The dark clouds rolled over one another, no doubt fighting over who would destroy us on our way back through. Lightning sprinted across them, leap-frogging each other like quick children.

I started when a figure appeared beside me. It was Xander, and he, too, looked out over the haunting view. However, I noticed his brow was furrowed a little too tight.

I nudged his arm with my elbow. "You okay?"

He shook himself and looked down at me, but I had a feeling he was more looking *through* me than *at* me. "Yes. I was merely admiring the view."

I arched an eyebrow. "You looked like you were in a trance."

It was his turn to raise a brow. "A trance?"

I shook my head before I looped my arm through one of his. "Never mind. Let's just go see this mistress and send her on her way."

The others waited for us halfway down the path that led from the arch to the pair of front doors. We stepped back in line, but Spiros sidled up to us and studied his old friend. "Are you feeling well?"

Xander nodded. "I am fine."

Spiros narrowed his eyes. "You look a little pale."

"I am fine."

We reached the doors and our guide grasped a nod before he turned to us with a smile. "Welcome to Echo Manor."

Abraxas opened the door and revealed to us a sweeping entrance hall of fine elegance and a penchant for clutter. Tapestries depicting dragons and fae covered the walls from floor to ceiling. Every bit of floor space against the walls was occupied by wispy bits of furniture that sported thin, elegantly-carved legs and tops with shimmering smooth surfaces of symmetrical designs.

There was also the mirrors. They hung from every conceivable part of the wall, even interrupting the tapestries so the cloth draped over them. The mirrors were large and small, square and thin. They hid in the deep frames beside the doors and proudly proclaimed their beauty in the centers of the walls. The mirrors granted no privacy. All was seen from a dozen different angles.

Tillit swept his eyes over the mirrors and wrinkled his snout. "And I thought the Red Dragons were conceited. This place makes a royal dressing room look like a lesson in modesty."

"Keep your wits about you," Spiros warned us.

Darda's eyes flickered to Tillit. "However much there is to be had."

Abraxas gestured to an elegant winding staircase that led upstairs. "If you would follow me."

He led us upstairs and revealed a long hallway that traveled the full length of the second floor. At our backs stood the tall, narrow windows, and in front of us was a long line of doors. A pair of doors occupied the prominent position in the center of the hall, and it was to those that Abraxas guided us.

He opened them and stepped aside, revealing a large bedroom chamber. A four-post bed took up the far right corner with a large stone fireplace on its left. A vanity and dresser were positioned against the left-hand wall. On either side of the fireplace were two large windows with thick curtains that blocked the light.

In the center of the room was a small table with two chairs. In one of those chairs, wrapped in a bundle of afghans, sat a small, wizened figure. It was a woman of great age whose face had wrinkles on top of wrinkles. Her long hair was pulled back in a tight bun atop her head. Beneath the blankets I could see a hint of a dress.

She beckoned to us with a hand as wrinkled as sand after the tide. "Please come in."

Xander led our group into the room. Abraxas slipped into the room and grasped the door knobs and shut the doors behind us, sealing us in the large room. A fire burned in the hearth, but warmth didn't reach us. I swept my eyes over the room and noticed there wasn't a speck of dust. Abraxas and his crew were apparently handy on shore.

"You are the mistress of this house?" Xander guessed.

The woman smiled and bowed her head to us. "Yes. You must excuse my not greeting you in more formal a manner. My body-" she gestured down at her withered form, "-is not as strong as it once was."

Xander arched an eyebrow. "I was not aware that gods aged."

She chuckled. "Most do not, but there is always an exception to the rule. *I* am that exception." She held out her hand to Xander. "But you must pardon my rudeness in not introducing myself. My name is Moneta, Mistress of Storms."

Xander took her hand and gave it a polite shake. "I am-"

"Xander, Lord of Alexandria," she finished for him. She slipped her hand from his hold and looked over our group one-by-one. "I see you have brought your captain, Spiros, Tillit, of the many travels, and your faithful servant,

Darda." Her eyes fell on me and her smile widened. "And of course your Maiden, Miriam of the other world."

Xander frowned. "How did you learn of our identities?"

"The wind brings much news. That is how I knew of your mission to banish my brethren from this world. Then, of course, I can feel it in these-" she raised one hand and turned the bony fingers over, "-these ancient bones of mine sense my brethren, and after each of your adventures I sensed they were gone from this world, or-" her eyes flickered to Spiros, "-at least from their fate as a steward of this world."

Tillit snorted. "If you're stewards than this world's doomed." Darda jabbed him in the side and glared at him.

Moneta chuckled. "I can see you have been speaking with Crates."

"You know him?" I spoke up.

She nodded. "Very well. We are old acquaintances, but that is a story for another time. Your journey was a long one, and I am sure you would like some rest."

"We have not forgotten our duty," Xander told her.

Moneta leaned back in her chair and smiled. "Ah yes, the duty to banish me." Her eyes fell on the bag strapped to my back. "No doubt you carry the chime with you at all times, but I can assure you there is no need of that with me. I mean you no harm, nor do I wish to harm this world."

"We cannot take that chance," Xander argued.

She gestured to the dark hall around us. "Is this the palace of a goddess intent on bending the world to her will? If you need more proof than ask my captain here-" she nodded at Abraxas who still stood beside the doors, "-how long the storm has carried on. How long *my* storm has been in existence, and I in its center."

"Twenty-thousand years," he informed us.

She nodded. "Yes. Twenty-thousand years of self-enforced solitude. I would know very little of the world if it was not for my sailors and their venturing out onto the seas and the coastlines. Then there is the winds that bring me news of the world and its events."

"You don't want us to use the chime," I surmised.

She bowed her head. "That is correct, or at the very least I would like you to wait a while before making your decision."

"Why would we wait?" Xander asked her.

A small, crooked smile slipped onto her lips. "I have isolated myself for so long because I have one last wish to grant myself."

"And what's that?" I questioned the goddess.

She chuckled. "That is a woman's secret."

"You're not expecting us to wait around for another twenty-thousand years, are you?" Tillit questioned her.

"No. I expect the wish to be fulfilled very soon. In the meantime-" she swept her hand over the room, "-I would be glad to have you as my guests. You will fill these long-empty rooms with much joy if you were to accept my invitation."

Xander pursed his lips and half-turned to us. His gaze fell on me. I shook my head and shrugged.

"I can sense your doubts as well as I can sense the air outside growing wilder," Moneta spoke up as she looked at each of us. "I see doubt in your faces, but you need not worry about me." She grasped the arms of her chair and eased herself to a standing position.

"My Lady!" Abraxas scolded her as he rushed forward with arms stretched out.

Moneta raised one hand to stop him from grasping her arms. He stopped a foot from her, and she looked past him at our group. Her body quivered as she gave us a small, shaky smile. "You have nothing to fear from this frail body. All I ask is a few days of your time, and then you may use the chime on me to banish me from this world."

I furrowed my brow and glanced up at Xander. His face showed his indecision, but finally he nodded. "We will allow you this time, but we will remain on our ship during our stay here."

Moneta bowed her head. "I thank you for your kindness, and will give kindness in return when the time comes."

CHAPTER 11

Moneta glanced at Abraxas. "Will you see to it that their hold is filled during their stay?"

Abraxas opened his mouth, but paused and tilted his head to one side as though listening. He furrowed his brow and narrowed his eyes. "I believe they will not be allowed that comfort, My Lady."

Our group tensed. Spiros set his hand on the hilt of his sword and glared at the dragon captain. "What do you mean by that?"

Abraxas walked over to the windows and drew aside the curtains. The glass was dirty, but we could see out across the short distance of the island to the seas. The sunny sky had grown cloudy and a rough wind drew white waves out of the waters. The spare weeds across the island bent under the will of the wind and the thin glass shivered as badly as their mistress.

Spiros whipped his head to Xander. "We should leave."

Xander gave a nod. "Yes."

Abraxas turned to our group and shook his head. "It is too late. The swells would overwhelm your small boat."

Xander took my hand and turned us toward the doors. "We will see."

Our group rushed from the room and through the decrepit house. We stepped out through the front doors and were greeted by a strong gust that threw me into the arms of my dragon lord. Darda stumbled to the side and into Tillit, who dug his heels in to keep both of them from falling into the thin brush.

"Easy there, my dear. You'll impale us both on those weeds if you're not careful," he teased.

The wind nearly took his words away on its rough gusts. The dark clouds completely covered the sun, casting the small world in thick shadows. The path that led to the docks was shrouded in darkness provided by the rocks and brush. An unforgiving rain soaked our clothes and pelted our faces with hard drops. I peered through the gloom and caught a glimpse of the dock. The waves crashed over the boards and shoved our little boat against the sides of the hard planks. Even from that distance I could hear the harsh knock of wood against wood.

Spiros bent his head against the brutal wind and glanced at Xander. "The wind has grown stronger since we looked out the window."

Abraxas came up behind us and grasped Xander's shoulder. "You cannot leave in this storm."

"We must see that our ship weathers this wind," Xander argued.

Abraxas looked out on the seas and nodded at a dark shape among the white caps. It was our ship. She bobbed in the rough seas like a cork, but the mermaid on her prow kept her head well above the waves. "Your ship is well-anchored.

DREAMS OF DRAGONS

She will hold against this storm. In the meanwhile, My Lady would be glad to hold you until the storm lets up."

Tillit came up behind him and looked the captain over. "Isn't she supposed to be controlling this storm?"

Abraxas nodded. "At most times, yes, but during heightened moments of emotion, such as your visiting, her control weakens and the storm gains in strength."

"That would've been nice to know before we came," I spoke up.

Xander glanced at me. "Would your powers allow you to guide us to the ship?"

I pursed my lips and shook my head. "I don't know. I can control the water, but not those winds."

The wind made its point when it blew against me, toppling me into Xander's arms. He grasped my shoulders and glanced at our companions. His voice was loud, but not clear as the gale swirled around us. "Everyone back inside!"

We scurried into the foyer, but the storm followed us. The wind swung the doors wide open, and only by the strength of Tillit, Spiros and Abraxas were they shut. The storm, angered at our escape, rattled the windows, but its fury was contained outside the thick walls.

Abraxas drew a heavy bolt across the doors and turned to us. "We will be safe within these walls. This house has stood against many a storm such as this and weathered it without many repairs."

My friends and I were soaked, but I wasn't bothered by the chilly water. While my clothes absorbed the moisture they left small puddles at their feet that reflected their bedraggled appearances.

Darda shivered and wrapped her arms around herself. "What a terrible storm."

Tillit clapped a hand on her back and the contact made a soft squishing noise. "You look like you're a bath in need of a bather, my dear Darda."

Abraxas gestured to the stairs. "Allow me to show you to your rooms."

Spiros narrowed his eyes at our guide. "That is very considerate of her since we were not expected to stay."

Abraxas smiled. "My Lady feared the worst would happen, and had them prepared. If you would follow me."

Tillit, Darda, and Spiros reluctantly followed him. Xander moved in front of me and I made to walk in his footsteps, but a soft sound came to my ears.

Miriam.

I paused and furrowed my brow. A man's voice. I was sure of it. I tilted my head to one side and concentrated, but there was only the push of the winds against the outside of the manor.

A hand touched my shoulder. I jumped and whipped my head up to look into the face of Xander. His worried eyes searched mine. "Are you well?"

I swept my eyes over the empty foyer. Nothing stirred. I ran a hand through my hair and shook my head. "I-I don't know. I swear I heard something."

He frowned. "What did you hear?"

I shrugged. "I thought it was a guy's voice, but I guess it was just my imagination."

"Is something the matter?" Spiros called from the banister halfway up the stairs.

I slapped a shaky smile on my lips. "It's fine. Just the storm playing tricks on me." Xander and Spiros believed it. I wished I could have, but doubt lingered in my mind.

We followed Abraxas upstairs to the long hall of the second floor. Contrary to his assurances the house was not as solid as he affirmed. The candles along the walls wavered and flickered against an inconsistent draft. Their lights danced across the walls and gave the impression of traveling through a troupe of dancers beckoning us to some forbidden revelry. He led us down the passage past many doors before we entered the west wing. The storm had added thunder and lightning to its resume so that great flashes of light flashed across the windows and illuminated the passage with their ghostly hue.

Abraxas stopped before a row of four doors and opened them one at a time. "I hope these will suffice."

I peeked inside the closest room and found a comfortable space. The floor was covered in thick rugs that softened and warmed bare feet. The four rooms shared two chimneys in the adjoining walls, and each stone chimney had a great awning hearth warmed by a crackling fire. Portraits of unknown people hung from the walls, and to the mix was added tapestries of forest and mountain scenes. The rooms were all the same but for the size of the bed in one which was double the others.

Abraxas gestured to the room with the exception. "This will be your room, My Lord and Lady. Your companions may choose any of the others for their use."

"What about food?" Tillit spoke up. Darda shot him a glare.

"My Lady wishes for you to join her for supper in an hour," Abraxas informed us. "The dining room is located downstairs and to the left of the stairs as you enter the house."

Spiros looked up and down the hall. "Are there any other servants here?"

Abraxas shook his head. "No. My crew and I are all that My Lady requires. If you will excuse me, I am on kitchen duty for this evening." He bowed his head and retreated down the hall the way we came.

Tillit stuck his head in one of the other bedrooms and wrinkled his nose. "Something smells fishy."

"That would be the sea," Darda quipped.

He turned to us and tapped the side of his nose. "This nose isn't just picking up on the water. This place smells like a place that's been boarded up for a decade and given over to the rats."

I lifted my nose in the air and took a whiff. "I don't smell anything."

"You just believe ol' Tillit. He knows what he's talking about," Tillit assured me.

Spiros sidled up to Xander's side and lowered his voice. "Whatever Tillit smells, I feel it in the air."

"As do I," Xander agreed as he glanced over his shoulder to look down the hall.

I looked past him at the end. The passage turned around a corner, but at the end stood a large window that looked out on the stormy island. The winds forced the clouds to roll over one another as though eager to pay homage to the lightning, but far afield I caught a glimpse of the second, smaller island.

Tillit squinted his eyes at the distant piece of land and frowned. "That's a bright island to be seeing it in this storm."

"Island or no island, we should prepare for dinner," Darda advised us as she grasped my shoulders and guided me into my shared room.

Tillit shrugged. "What for? We might be the main course."

Darda paused and looked over her shoulder to glare at him. "She is a goddess, not a man-eater."

He grinned and gave her a wink. "Anybody with that much beauty left might be both."

Spiros turned Tillit away from Darda so he avoided her scorching look. "Wise advise, Darda. Let me help you wash up, Tillit."

Darda turned up her nose and looked back at me, but her words were for the pair of men. "Do not forge to dunk him in the bowl. He may improve with washing."

Spiros pushed Tillit inside before the sus could fire another shot and shut the door firmly behind them. Darda looped one arm around that of Xander and drew him toward the door. "You should not remain in this drafty hall, Xander."

DREAMS OF DRAGONS

He shook himself from his fascination with the other island and allowed himself to be led into the room. A vanity stood on our left, and on its top sat a pitcher and bowl for washing. These were daily reminders of how much I missed indoor plumbing. I walked over to the bed and took a seat at the foot. The backpack, soaked and heavy, slid off my back and gave my weary self a little reprieve.

CHAPTER 12

The position gave me a good view of the room. The dark wall panels were illuminated by the candelabras that hung on either side of the door and the vanity mirror. Their soft light cast deep shadows over the two portraits that hung on the wall opposite the foot of the bed, deepening the skill of the artist by adding depth to the paint. The portraits were that of a man and woman, but time had taken its toll so that beyond the dress and suit the details weren't clear, particularly their faces. The effect gave one the impression they were headless.

"Nice place. . ." I muttered as I looked away from the creepy portraits.

Xander stepped up to the doorway and ran his hand down the ancient wood. "How very curious. . ."

I snorted. "You mean besides us staying in a creepy old house during a huge storm with a goddess that might be serving us poison in an hour?"

DREAMS OF DRAGONS

He tilted his head to one side as he studied the wood and shook his head. "No."

I leaned my hands behind me on the bed and arched an eyebrow. "None of that bothers you?"

Xander dropped his hand and turned to me. "I am as troubled as you are about those things, but until the challenge of consuming poison arrives I find myself very perplexed by this house."

I glanced up at the open-rafter ceiling with its thick, sturdy beams. The floor beneath my feet was as solid as stone, and the windows held back the torrential rain that pelted their glass. "It seems sturdy to me."

He nodded. "That is what troubles me."

Darda frowned at him. "How can that trouble you?"

Xander walked over and stopped beside one of the four posts of the bed and set his hand against the wood. "The goddess told us that she had exiled herself for twenty-thousand years and her only contact was in the ancient sailors of Alexandria, yet we sit within a house that appears to have been built only a few years ago." He pursed his lips and shook his head. "I cannot see how both can be true."

"The sailors of Alexandria would be well-versed in repairing wood," Darda pointed out.

"That may be true, but they would need supplies to repair any damage caused by age," he countered.

I stood and shrugged. "Maybe she oils everything really well with poison and that-"

A flash of lightning traveled across the sky just outside the windows and the booming thunder followed its mate. The glass shook against the harsh reverberations of nature's wrath. The flimsy clasp that held the winged windows closed sprung open and the glass flew into the room and hit the wall. Some of the panes shattered, spilling rain and glass across the floor. The wild wind blew out the candles, engulfing the room in darkness accentuated by shadows.

Miriam.

That voice again. The sound made my blood run cold. I whipped my head around, but I saw nothing but shadows. Flickering, twisting shadows.

Darda rushed over to me and wrapped me in her arms. I could feel the narrow bodies of her daggers concealed in her cloak. Xander ran over to the window and shut the windows. He secured the clasp and stopped the downpour, but the rain slipped in through the broken panes and soaked the glass-ridden rug.

The door swung open and Spiros and Tillit vied with one another to be the first. The spry captain won and hurried over to Xander while Tillit joined Darda and me. He grasped Darda's arm and looked us over. "We heard something break. Are you all right?"

Darda nodded. "Yes. It was merely the faulty latch on the window."

Spiros' eyes flickered from the latch to Xander's pensive expression. The dragon lord's gaze lay locked on the clasp. "Was it the wind?"

Xander raised his hand and moved the clasp from shut to locked. The latch moved stiffly beneath his hand. He looked to his captain and pursed his lips. "I am not sure."

"I'm sure that we should be getting out of this room, and maybe this house," Tillit spoke up.

I remained fixed on that voice. It had called to me, and I'd felt a strange urge to follow where it led. I couldn't have imagined that feeling. Could I?

Darda leaned forward and caught my gaze. "Are you well, Miriam?" Everyone's focus fell on me.

Xander strode over and grasped my arms as he searched my face. "What is the matter?"

I shook myself and gave him a smile. "I'm fine."

He narrowed his eyes. "You look unwell. Your face is pale."

DREAMS OF DRAGONS

I shrugged myself free of his grasp and shook my head. "I just heard something funny in the wind, that's all."

"I didn't hear you laughing," Tillit spoke up.

"What did you hear?" Xander questioned me.

I turned my face away from his prying eyes and pursed my lips. "I. . .I thought I heard someone calling me."

Tillit jerked a thumb at Darda. "Old battle-ax here?"

Darda glared at him. "I did not call her."

"It wasn't Darda. I-" I bit my lower lip and wrapped my arms around myself. The room was cold from the broken window, but the chill sank deeper than my skin. "I don't know who it was, but it sounded familiar. And I. . .I. . ."

"You had the urge to follow its call," a voice spoke up.

Everyone spun around to face the door. In their rush to enter Tillit and Spiros had left it ajar, and now Abraxas stood in the doorway.

I nodded. "Yeah, but how'd you know that?"

He stepped into the room and fixed his eyes on me. "It would be better if My Lady explained the situation to you. She awaits your presence in the dining room."

Spiros looked to Xander who nodded. My dragon lord set his hand on the lower part of my back and guided me toward the door. Abraxas left first, and our friends followed behind us out into the long hall.

Xander leaned toward me and lowered his voice to a whisper. "What did this voice say to you?"

"Only my name," I told him.

"A man or woman?"

"Man."

"And familiar to you?" I nodded. He leaned away and pursed his lips, but his hand kept a tight pressure against my lower back as we were led down to the dining hall.

The long room lay in the western wing below our rooms. A large chandelier dangled from the ceiling and illuminated the hardwood panel walls and polished floor. To

79

our left stood the long front wall of the house, and the many windows granted us a grand view of the storm as it thrashed the water with its winds.

A wide table stretched to nearly the full fifty feet of the room, and at one end were set enough places for everyone. The china was of the finest, and plates brimming with meats, cheeses, and vegetables were already laid.

Moneta herself sat at the head of the table. There was no plate in front of her, but she held a glass of wine in one shriveled hand. She smiled at our coming and bowed her head to us. "I hope you have brought an appetite. I eat very little myself, but I am able to provide a good fair for guests."

Abraxas walked up to her side and half-bowed to her. "My Lady, there is a problem."

She leaned back and arched an eyebrow as she looked up at him. "What sort of problem?"

He nodded at him. "This young woman-"

"Miriam," she reminded him.

He nodded. "Yes, Miriam, she has heard a voice calling to her."

Moneta pursed her lips and turned her attention to me. "I see."

"I wish I did," I quipped.

Our hostess set her glass on the table and leaned back in her tall chair. "It is a long story." She gestured to the set places. "If you would sit I will tell you all that I remember, for this is an old tale."

We reluctantly walked around the table to our seats. Xander guided me behind our hostess for the prime right-hand spot, but she grasped his hand as he passed her and smiled up at him.

"I would much prefer your lovely Maiden be seated on my right, My Lord," she pleaded. She gestured to the seat that lay empty on her left. "You may sit there."

He shook his head. "I would rather-"

"Please. This story is very important for her well-being." Her eyes flickered to me. Their depths held an emotion I couldn't decipher, but one which made my blood run cold. "Nay, possibly even her life."

"That is why I wish to remain close to her," Xander argued.

Moneta smiled at him as she took one of my hands and guided me out of his hold. "She will be safe beside me. I will guarantee it."

Xander pursed his lips and glanced across the table. Darda sidled up beside the place of honor and grasped her hip. She wasn't injured. At her hip was a small holster of her daggers. Xander looked down at Moneta and nodded.

Our hostess's face brightened. "Very good. Now if you will all take your seats I will begin."

CHAPTER 13

"My story begins twenty-thousand years ago when I came to this fine house," she began as she gestured to the walls around us. The storm battered them and the wind beat them, but they held against its fury. "The manor was new at that time, a work of beauty by an eccentric sailor who had made his fortune in trade. I. . .I purchased the island from him, though the companion to this island was owned by another. It was that other who brought down the curse upon this island."

"What curse?" I asked her.

She sighed. "The curse of memories." Our group glanced at one another. A small smile slipped onto her pale lips. "I know that means nothing to you, but to me that is my life. I am so immersed in these memories that nothing is beyond them."

"What is the nature of this curse?" Xander wondered.

DREAMS OF DRAGONS

She sat up and entwined her fingers together in front of her. "The curse grants one the ability to see those they once knew, but they are mere phantoms. Ghosts, if you would."

Tillit, with his plate piled high but untouched, leapt to his feet. "I think that's our cue to leave."

The storm decided to chime in with its opinion. A streak of lightning shot across the sky followed by a thundering boom that shook the whole house.

Spiros, who sat beside him, pulled him back into his seat. "If we leave now *we* would become the ghosts."

Moneta nodded. "Yes. The storm is against you."

I leaned toward her and eyed our hostess. "Can't you stop it?"

She shook her head. "Not on this night. I used all my powers to guide you through its rough winds, but now-" she leaned back and closed her eyes. "Now I am too weak to bid the storm cease the rain, much less the great winds."

"Then we are at the mercy of the storm and spirits?" Darda spoke up.

Moneta creaked open her eyes and they fell on each of us, one at a time. "I fear so, but all is not lost. The memories may choose to leave you alone, at least until we can get you safely to your ship."

"But I've already heard them," I reminded her.

Her gaze fell on me and her hand slid over to settle atop one of mine. Her touch was as cold as ice. "You have your friends to protect you and, my people willing, they will keep you safe through the night."

"Why did this person bring a curse on your house?" Xander spoke up.

Moneta withdrew her hand and shook her head. "There was once when I could answer that question, but time has robbed me of much. I can only assure you that none of it was my doing." Another flash of lightning ripped across the sky followed by its inevitable thundering boom. The mood was dire. The food untouched, even by Tillit.

The sus sighed and picked up his fork. "Well, I guess we should enjoy our last meal."

Darda tapped a finger against her knife as she glared at him. "You lose hope far too quickly, Mr. Tillit."

Tillit dug into a helping of mashed potatoes and shrugged. When he spoke it was with a full mouth and spraying of food. "Hope is what somebody does when they don't know what's going to happen next. I know what's going to happen."

All eyes fell on him. Our hostess raised her chin a little and arched an eyebrow. "You do?"

He swallowed and nodded. "Yep. Trouble."

A small smile slipped onto Moneta's lips as she leaned back. "I see. Well, I will try to make this visit of yours as uneventful as-"

A strong gust blew against the windows. The thin panes of glass rattled and several of the latches were brushed aside, flinging the windows open and allowing rain to pour in. The wind rushed inside and blew around the room like an unwelcome house guest. It extinguished the candles, plunging us into a deep darkness, but not silence. Our company shouted and a few glasses toppled over as we slid our chairs back. I felt Darda grasp my arm like a boa constrictor.

The men leapt from their seats and the sailors hurried from a side door from the kitchen. With their joined efforts the windows were shut and secured, though the floor was soaked and the cloth on the dining table sported several wine stains.

I glanced at our hostess. "I think-" My words caught in my throat.

She was gone. The seat formerly occupied by Moneta now stood empty.

DREAMS OF DRAGONS

"My Lord!" Darda shouted, her loss of composure forcing her back into old habits.

The men turned to face us, and their eyes widened. Abraxas rushed over to the empty chair and gasped the arm. "My Lady!" He whipped his head around the room, but his search was futile. "My Lady!" His call echoed over the room, but only his own voice replied.

"Where could she have gone?" Xander asked the distraught captain.

Abraxas shook his head. "I cannot fathom it. She is far too frail to disappear on her own power."

"Could the memories have stolen her away?" Spiros suggested.

Abraxas pursed his lips. "That is possible. They are at their most powerful during these terrible storms."

Tillit came up to their little group and arched an eyebrow. "Why these storms?"

The captain stood straight and shook his head. "That is not for me to say, nor do I feel inclined when My Lady has been kidnapped and must be found."

"I will offer my services and those of my companions in the search," Xander offered.

Abraxas nodded. "We would be much obliged for any help. This is a large house and a thorough search will take quite some time, especially in this dark."

Xander turned to Darda and me. "We will take the second floor."

Tillit grinned at Spiros. "That leaves you and me with-" he paused and furrowed his brow before he looked to Abraxas. "What does that leave us?"

"My men and I will search the grounds and the ground floor, which leaves only the third floor to be searched," Abraxas told him.

Tillit clapped his hand on Spiros's shoulder. "You heard the captain, sailor. Off we go."

I held up my hands. "Wait a sec." The entire company paused and turned to me. "Exactly what are we dealing with here? I mean, what are these things capable of doing besides talking to me and dragging off an ancient woman?"

The captain pursed his lips. "There is no limit to the trickery for the memories in this ancient home, but so long as you remain together they should not harm you."

Tillit snorted. "That didn't help your lady."

"She is frail and the windows distracted all of our attentions," Abraxas pointed out. "Remain alert and together, and we shall find her in very little time."

Xander nodded. "We will find her." He turned to our group. "Let us begin."

Anxiety and apprehension were my two companions as we headed for the stairs. The candles were still lit in the other rooms so that furniture wasn't an obstacle, but my emotions weren't helping me. We climbed the first flight of stairs to the second floor landing.

I grasped Xander's sleeve and gave a tug, stopping him in his tracks so he could look over his shoulder at me. The long hall echoed so that I lowered my voice to a whisper to avoid being overheard by the downstairs searchers. "You sure this is such a good idea?"

He shook his head. "No, but I cannot see that we have any other choice. All our answers, and our purpose in being here, lies with finding the goddess."

Tillit patted the pack on my back. "And singing a sweet tune to her."

Darda swatted away his hand. "Do not announce such secrets to everyone in the world."

He cradled his injured hand in his other palm and shrugged. "They're going to know sooner or later."

"And it will be much later if you do not start your search," she scolded him.

DREAMS OF DRAGONS

Spiros opened his arm to invite Tillit with him up the next flight of stairs. "Come on, Tillit, before you become our second disappearance."

The pair walked up the other flight and their footsteps faded away on the thick floor boards above our heads. I sighed and glanced over my two remaining companions. Darda rested one hand on the top handle of what I guessed was a dagger and she glared at where Tillit had gone. Xander's eyes lay down the long hall which had captured his attention so thoroughly earlier.

I tugged on his sleeve. He started and looked down at me. His face showed a tension that frightened me. "You okay?"

He shook himself. "I am not sure."

I glanced down the dark hall and nodded at the corner. "Is something down there?"

Xander slipped his arm around my back and tightly gripped my waist. "We shall see."

CHAPTER 14

We strode down the hall, our pairs of feet tapping against the bare floorboards. Outside the storm continued to throw a tantrum as though it knew its mistress had been stolen away by unknown forces. As we came closer to the corner of the hall Xander's stride slowed until he stopped a few yards from the end.

"Xander?" I asked him as I slipped in front of him and studied his face. His face was pale and his eyes were riveted to the corner. "Xander, are you okay?"

He didn't reply. I snapped my fingers in front of his face. He started back and blinked down at me. His lips parted and a soft whisper escaped them. "Miriam. . ."

I crossed my arms over my chest and glared at him. "It's nice to know you haven't forgotten about me completely."

Darda slipped up on his side and glanced from Xander to the corner. "Is something amiss, My Lord?"

DREAMS OF DRAGONS

I leaned back and furrowed my brow as I caught Xander's gaze. "You saw a memory, didn't you?"

He raised his eyes to the corner and pursed his lips. "Perhaps."

Darda frowned. "My Lord, 'perhaps' tells us very little."

Xander shook himself and gave us an unconvincing smile. "You are right, Darda. The storm may be playing tricks on my eyes, and now." He turned to the long row of doors. They totaled about two dozen and were all shut to our prying eyes. "We have a great many rooms to search."

My eyes flickered between my companions. "This might be a stupid question, but should we search them together or apart?"

"I will search alone so long as you two are together," Darda offered.

"Are you sure?" he asked her.

She bowed her head. "Yes. My daggers and I will be fine."

Xander nodded at the opposite end of the hall. "Then you will begin there and we will start here. If you hear or see anything, avoid confrontation and hurry into the hall."

"I will, Xander." Darda turned and walked down the hall. She opened the last door and disappeared inside.

I turned to the door closest to us and the corner that so enraptured Xander. Xander stepped up to the door and opened the portal. The room was another bedroom, but not like ours. Cobwebs and dust covered the white sheets that hid the furniture from our eyes. The ghostly attire of the furniture was illuminated by a flash of lightning across the filthy windows that stood opposite us.

Xander stepped inside and swept his eyes around the room. I moved to follow, but something out of the corner of my eye caught my attention. It was a flash of color in the otherwise dark hall, and it came from the corner. I pressed one hand against the wall to my right and crept toward the end of the hall.

Another flash of lightning lit up the corridor, giving me a clear view of the dark shadows that hid the corner. My eyes widened as I beheld a change in the hall. The clean windows and the papered walls vanished, and in their places was decay. The walls were broken down to jagged spikes and gave a terrifyingly broad view of the violent seas. Ancient glass covered in dust lay strewn about rotten floorboards.

I covered my mouth with one hand and took a step back. A hand fell on my shoulder. I screamed and spun around. Xander stood before me. His worried eyes searched mine. "What is it?" he asked me. He raised his gaze to the corner and pursed his lips. "You saw it."

I furrowed my brow. "Saw 'it?'"

He grasped my upper arms and nodded without looking at me. "Yes. The ruins of this house. It is why I suspect there is more occurring here than our hostess has told us."

My eyes widened. "Then you saw what I just saw?"

He nodded. "Yes. The lightning has repeatedly revealed the scene for me. I thought perhaps I was mistaken, but-" he returned his attention to me and studied my face, "-I can see that you, too, have seen the ruin."

"But what does it mean?" I asked him.

He shook his head. "I do not know, but for now we should answer the question of our missing hostess." He made to step back into the cloth-covered room, but I grabbed his arm and caught his eyes with mine.

"What if whatever got her is worse than a god? And the chime doesn't work on it?" I wondered.

Xander turned to face me and clasped my hands in his. "Whatever troubles will come our way I believe we will overcome them."

DREAMS OF DRAGONS

I sighed and glanced at the gloomy room. "I hope you're-" The words froze in my throat as my heart froze in my chest.

Xander furrowed his brow as he studied me. "Is something the matter?"

I pointed a shaking finger at a long, covered sofa. "I-it moved."

My dragon lord frowned and released me. He grasped the hilt of his sword and strode over to the furniture. I took a step into the room, but paused just beyond the threshold. Xander threw off the sheet and revealed an overstuffed sofa with a hideous flowered pattern. All that moved in his reveal was a thick layer of dust. The fluffy dirt settled over the room as a mist. A flash of lightning reflected off the tiny specks and created a dazzling display of refraction that clouded the room.

Movement to my right caught my attention. I whipped my head in the direction of the four-post bed. Several layers lay of sheets over the mattress. One of those layers floated up into the form of an upright human body.

"Xander!" I shouted.

Xander drew out his sword and rushed to my side. The sheet slid off the foot of the bed and floated toward us. I let out a shriek as Xander leapt forward and slashed the sheet-and its occupant-in twain. The sheet fell away, but not what lay beneath.

A man stood before us. His form was transparent and his pale flesh glowed in the dim light. His clear eyes, devoid of emotion, were fixed on me. My hand flew to my mouth to stifle my gasp.

"Dad!"

The figure that floated in front of us was indeed that of my father. My *long-dead* father.

"Mother!" Xander whispered.

I whipped my head to him and frowned. "Mother? Xander, that's my dad!"

Xander backed up with uncertainty on his face. He clenched his sword tighter in his hand and his eyes flickered over his shoulder at me. "I see only my mother."

I waved my hand at my floating father. "How can you think that's your mom?"

Footsteps pounded in the corridor and Darda rushed inside. She clapped her hands on her cheeks and let out a shriek at the sight of the spooky specter. "Lord Alexander!"

I blinked at her. "Lord? That's my dad?"

Xander stepped up to my side and narrowed his eyes at our unwelcome visitor. "There is something amiss here."

I snorted. "I'll say. You're both going blind."

He glanced at our friend. "Remove Miriam from this room." Darda wrapped her arms around one of mine and tugged me toward the door.

I yanked myself free from her hold and glared at both of them. "I'm not going anywhere while my father-" I waved at the apparition, "-is floating just a few feet from me."

Xander shook his head. "I do not believe this is your father any more than I believe this is my mother."

"But he is the image of your father!" Darda insisted.

More footsteps warned us of impending confusion, and soon Tillit and Spiros-both covered in thick layers of dust-rushed into the room. They slid to a stop just inside the doorway and both gaped at the figure

"Father!" Spiros gasped.

Tillit's mouth opened slightly and he blinked at the ghost. "Mom?"

I threw up my arms. "Who *isn't* this thing?"

Xander sheathed his weapon and studied the figure carefully. "I believe this creature is a phantom."

"How does that make it different than a ghost?" I asked him.

"A phantom just pretends to be a spook," Tillit told me. He rubbed his chin in one hand as he studied the creature before us. "Now that I think about it, my mom

DREAMS OF DRAGONS

wouldn't be found dead in a place like this. She much preferred the docks of Didymes than the grand mansions along that lake."

Xander took a step toward the figure, but I grabbed his arm. "What are you going to do?"

"Dispel the creature if I can," he told me.

I pursed my lips and my eyes flickered to the floating spirit. "Is there. . .couldn't we prove it's not a ghost first? Just in case?"

Spiros glanced at Tillit and his ever-present bag. "Is there anything within your satchel that might help us?"

Tillit furrowed his brow. "If I remember correctly-" his eyes lit up, "-that's it!" He plopped his bag on the ground and knelt before the container. The sus buried his face deep into the bag and burrowed his way through any number of strange gadgets and trinkets.

I glanced at the ghost. The figure hovered there with its eyes still fixed on me. Its gaze seemed to penetrate my soul. A faint voice floated over the air like a feather falling to the ground.

Miriam.

I shuddered and looked away. Xander was right, this couldn't be my dad. He wouldn't frighten me so much.

"Here we are," Tillit spoke up as he lifted a small gong from his bag. The gong hung from a wooden dowel and in the dim light I could make out a few inscriptions etched into the wood.

Darda frowned at the musical instrument. "What are we to do with such a thing? Torture the creature with your music?"

"Not just my music, my dear Darda, but everyone's music," Tillit told her as he slung his bag back over his shoulder. "This little trinket is something I picked up on Phantasma Insula-"

"That is a forbidden island!" Darda scolded him.

He grinned. "Yeah, but not for the tourists. This here-" he raised the gong in his hand, "is something the tour guides hand out in case one of the phantoms gets a little too friendly."

"What's this place?" I asked them.

"The Island of the Phantoms," Spiros translated for me. "Five thousand years ago two native tribes of naga made war upon one another for the island. They destroyed each other down to the last child. Now only their spirits remain as phantoms, creatures jealous of the living who are capable of leading them to their own deaths."

"But how could such a thing be here?" Darda wondered.

Xander pursed his lips as he studied the creature that looked like my dad. "There have been instances where a phantom was captured in a bottle and removed from the island."

"Let's just see if this thing's one of those phantoms or just a plain ghost," Tillit announced.

Tillit raised the gong and flicked his fingers against the metal. A tiny twinkling gong echoed around the room. I heard a groan and looked back at the ghost. The creature leaned its head back and loosed another deep, guttural groan. Its figure flickered like an old television where it was losing picture.

Spiros glanced at Tillit. "What does this prove?"

Tillit lowered the instrument and grinned at the phantom. "It means all I see now is a shadows, so this spook is no spook." He held out the gong to Spiros. "See for yourself."

Spiros took the instrument and clanged his fingers against the side. The phantom groaned again, louder this time, and it clapped its hands over its ears.

Spiros nodded. "I see what you mean. It is nothing more than a shadow."

DREAMS OF DRAGONS

He handed the gong over to Darda who rang the gong. The phantom floated back to the foot of the bed and writhed in pain. Its mouth opened to a silent cry of anguish as it clutched its head in its hands. Xander was the next to sound its destruction, and the phantom stepped back into its sheet. Its feet were partially absorbed by the cloth and its body was so clear I could see the details of the bed.

I started back when Xander brushed the gong against my shoulder. He caught my eyes and held out the instrument to me. I took the impromptu weapon with a shaking hand and a pain in my gut. The phantom lowered its hands and its eyes-those cold, death-like things-fell back on me. I raised the gong and inched my fingers close to its hard surface.

That's when the phantom rushed me.

CHAPTER 15

Xander wrapped his arm around me and drew me out of its path. The phantom floated past us and through the wall. Everyone breathed a sigh of relief that was punctuated by a flash of lightning and another clap of thunder.

Tillit backed up and swept his wide eyes over the room. His face was a little pale and I noticed his hand that clutched the strap of his bag shook. "This is not good."

Xander kept a tight hold on me as he looked over at Tillit. "What do you mean?"

Tillit swallowed the lump in his throat. "When somebody makes a phantom mad the phantom does some-" A screech like that of a banshee interrupted his words.

The sound cut through my ears and reverberated inside my head. I clapped my hands over my ears and cringed as my companions did the same. The phantom appeared through the door, but it was no longer my father. The creature was dressed in a black robe from collar to floating feet, and over its head was a dark hood. It flew at me with its hands outstretched. They were all bone, no flesh. I threw up my arms in front of me to protect myself and felt its icy touch on my skin.

I shut my eyes for only a second, and when I opened them the room was gone. All around me was a thick, drifting fog. The white mist brushed against my skin and chilled me to the bone. I wrapped my arms around myself and shivered.

"Xander?" I called out. My voice vanished into the mist. "Darda? Spiros? Tillit? You there?"

I took a step forward and the mist parted a little to reveal a forest. Thick, ancient trees loomed up all around me, their trunks surrounded by sparse bushes choked of sun by the towering Goliaths. Leaves, long abandoned by their parents, crunched beneath my foot as a slight breeze blew across me.

There was another crunch of leaves, but not from my feet. I squinted into the thick fog as the mist swirled around me.

A figure flew out of the darkness at a quick sprint. I started back as I recognized my father, and in his arms was cradled a small babe. Me. I took a step forward and the leaves crumpled beneath my feet.

"Dad?" I called out. He rushed past me without slowing. I spun around and watched him take a hard left at a large tree and continue onward. "Dad!"

I sprinted after him, following him step-for-step. My heart pounded in my chest and my legs beneath me as we raced through the woods. I was catching him. In a few moments I'd have him, so I quickened my speed to make that time come faster.

A pair of arms wrapped around my waist and lifted me off the ground. My feet kicked the air as the rest of me thrashed in their hold.

"Let me go!"

"Not on your life, Miriam," Tillit's voice replied as he tightened his grip on me. "Because that's exactly what it'll be if I let you go."

I gazed out ahead of us. My father's retreating back was nearly gone. I stretched out my hand to him. "Dad! Wait!"

He disappeared, and with him went the fog. The area around me cleared and I found myself in the corridor of the old house. A flash of lightning outside illuminated a harrowing discovery.

I was only three steps away from rushing headlong into the window at the end of the hall.

"I was wondering if I could put you down," Tillit wheezed behind me as he readjusted his hold around my waist. "You're small, but not that small."

"I-I'm okay," I told him. Tillit set me down on my shaky legs and I half-turned to him. "Thank you for saving my life."

He shrugged. "It was nothing. I'm just glad I got to you before you became a phantom."

I looked past him and down the hall. The corridor was empty but for we two. "Where's everyone else?"

Tillit pursed his lips and glanced over his shoulder. "They're still trapped by the phantom. I thought with you running out like that that you'd be in worse trouble than the others."

"Trapped how?"

He tapped his temple. "The phantom likes to play tricks on your mind. It'll show you stuff from your past and try to get you to kill yourself so it won't be alone."

"But you weren't affected?" I guessed.

He grinned and tapped the side of his nose. "The smells in these phantom dreams aren't the same as the real stuff, so one whiff told me I wasn't on the shores of Didymes Limnes." A clash of steel returned our attention to the open bedroom door at the opposite end of the hall. "Xander!"

I ran down the hall with Tillit in close pursuit. We came to the door and paused on the threshold. Our three friends were still in the room, but they were in trouble. Spiros and Xander were caught in a duel with their swords while Darda lay on the bed curled into a fetal position. She rocked herself to and fro in time with the clash of the swords as the swordsmen tried to deal a death-blow to the other.

"I will not allow you to live, Red Dragon!" Xander shouted.

"You will pay for murdering my father!" Spiros replied.

"Are they hearing the same conversation?" I asked Tillit.

He shook his head. "I don't think so. You take Xander and I'll see what I can do with our good captain."

We slipped behind our fighting comrades. I raised my hands and small tendrils of water slipped out. At a nod from Tillit I shot them forward. At the same time, Tillit literally jumped Spiros, landing on his back and shoving him to the floor.

Xander's sword clattered to the ground as he thrashed in my hold. "Release me!"

"Not until you wake up," I returned.

"I must kill the Red Dragon! I must!"

I slapped a tendril across his cheek. His head jerked to one side and his eyes widened. They blinked a few times before he shook his head and swept his eyes over the room.

"The manor?" he whispered.

"And the Maiden," I quipped as I walked up to his side. My tendrils still held him in place. "Are you okay now?"

He nodded. "I believe so." I released him from my bondage and he rubbed his head. "What happened?"

I gestured to Spiros who lay face-first on the floor with Tillit atop him. "That phantom was making you duel Spiros."

"And Spiros would be much obliged if a certain sus would get off him," came the mumbled reply of the captain.

"I'm comfortable," Spiros returned with a grin.

"You are not at all light," Spiros retorted.

Tillit chuckled, but stood and helped Spiros to his feet. A groan from the corner caught our attention. Darda lay atop the sheets nestled into a ball.

"Please let me go home," she whimpered. "Please. I promise I won't tell anyone about the portal."

"What's she talking about?" I asked my companions.

Xander pursed his lips. "She is reliving her capture in our world." He strode toward her, but Tillit rushed up to him and grabbed his wrist.

"A moment, My Lord," Tillit requested as he picked up the gong from the ground where I'd dropped it at the phantom's attack. He held it out to me. "One more gong should get rid of this annoyance."

I took the gong and marched up to Darda. My shadow fell over her face. She recoiled and squished herself against the wall.

"P-please don't hurt me!" she pleaded.

I raised the gong and snapped my finger against the metal. The sweet song floated over the room. A dark shadow floated up from Darda's body and formed itself into a balloon-shaped head as black as the darkest shadow. Its eyes widened and it opened its bottomless mouth in a horrible wail. The sound was stifled as the head faded into nothing.

Darda stopped shivering and raised her head to look at me. "Miriam?"

Tillit took the gong from me before I sat on the bed beside her. "Hey there. Have a bad dream?"

DREAMS OF DRAGONS

She sat up and winced before she rubbed her head. "I. . .I believe so."

Spiros turned to Xander. "How shall we go about in this search with such dangers?"

Xander shook his head. "I do not know, but splitting up is no longer a wise idea."

I opened my mouth to chime in agreement, but movement out of the corner of my eyes caught my attention. My eyes flickered to the left where another dusty portrait adorned the wall. This was of a man in old attire with a cravat around his neck and white fluff coming out of the long sleeves of his shirt.

His face captured my focus and quickened my heartbeat. The features were slim with a cruel curl of the lips. His eyes were narrow and as hard as stone. I squinted as I tried to make out their color.

The eyes blinked. I started back and did my own blinking. A hand settled on my shoulder.

"Is something the matter?" Darda asked me.

I shook my head. "No."

Tillit snorted. "I think we've had enough of 'nothing's-the-matter-but-it-really-is" for a lifetime, now tell us what's bothering you."

I nodded at the portrait. "I thought I saw that painting move."

Spiros picked up his sword from the floor where Tillit's weight had knocked it and strode over to the painting. He raised the weapon and tapped the tip of the sword against the heavy canvas. The cloth gave beneath before the point and the tip poked a hole through the man's chest.

My mouth dropped open as I watched a stream of black blood flow from the 'wound.' The subject's face contorted with pain and anger. Those dark eyes came alive with malice and jealousy. Spiros jerked his sword back, but the man's hand shot out and grabbed the blade. Blood dripped from his hand and onto the floor where it pooled into a puddle of ink.

The figure leaned forward and broke the fourth wall as he extended beyond the borders of the painting. He opened his mouth wide and revealed two rows of sharp, pointed teeth eager to bite into Spiros's neck. Spiros slammed his elbow into the man's face, shoving him back and allowing the captain to yank the sword from his hold.

Spiros stumbled back to us as the room became alive with movement. Cloths hung over another half a dozen portraits, but they were tossed aside by their subjects. Men and women, and even a scene of satyrs stretched out their hands toward us.

"Time to leave!" Tillit shouted.

CHAPTER 16

Spiros took the lead while Xander shoved the rest of us behind him. The subjects grasped the wood paneling on the walls and drew themselves from their paintings. Those drawn without legs were cropped at the artist's discretion while the satyrs, flutes a-playing, leapt out fully formed. They raced toward us and unsheathed the pointed wooden stakes at their waists.

Xander fended them off as we raced into the corridor. He shoved them back and slammed the door behind him. Many hands pounded on the door and the handle rattled like a snake.

"We must barricade ourselves in our room!" Darda insisted.

Tillit snorted. "Did you see how many paintings were in that one?"

"Did anyone notice a room without paintings?" Spiros asked us.

"The dining hall," Tillit suggested.

Xander shook his head. "We could not protect a room with that many windows."

My eyes widened. "The throne room! There weren't any portraits there!"

A sharp stake stabbed through the door and nicked Xander in the shoulder. He cried out and clutched his arm as blood swelled from the wound. I hurried to his side and drew him away from the entrance. A wave of my hand and a wall of water was thrown up in front of the door. The entrance swung inward and revealed our menagerie of foes. The satyrs at the front stepped toward us, but stopped at the wall. The creatures opened their mouths and let loose a shrill shriek that rattled the windows.

A heavy clump of footsteps warned us of more trouble. I whipped my head in the direction of the staircase. Shadows fell across the floor and climbed up the wall. The owners of those shadows appeared, and my blood ran cold as I saw they were the other members of the painting society come to greet us.

"Everyone stand back!" Tillit shouted as he dropped his bag to the floor.

The sus dug into its contents like a feverish badger as Spiros pulled us behind him. Darda stepped up to his side and drew out a half dozen of her daggers. His eyes flickered to her weapons. "Can those injure these creatures?"

She swept her eyes over his own sword. "Can yours?"

He raised his sword and grinned. "We shall see."

The pair rushed forward into the den of depictions. Their weapons cut through the paper apparitions like hot knives through butter, and the subjects fell to the floor in ribbons dashed with blood ink. Each swing of their weapons, however, created a hydra as the cuts of paper people rose from the floor and leapt at them.

DREAMS OF DRAGONS

Darda and Spiros stepped back and surveyed the army that now stood before them. The captain pursed his lips. "We are only making matters worse."

Darda, her brow covered in sweat, nodded. "Yes, but we have no other choice."

"Look out!" Tillit announced as he drew himself out of the bag. Darda and Spiros spun around in time to watch Tillit's arms come out. He held in them the infamous bat cannon.

Darda's eyes widened. "Not that!"

Tillit hefted the cannon in both hands with the back tucked under one arm. He pointed the wide mouth at the army of paintings. Our two friends stood in the line of fire. Spiros grabbed Darda and threw them both to the ground as Tillit fired the cannon. The resounding crash echoed up and down the corridor, making orphans of all the glass as they were shattered from the windows.

The vampiri de hârtie flew at top speed on their paper wings and peppered our equally papered foes. Screeching bats met screeching fiends as the paper creatures made war upon one another, scratching and clawing each other like a frenzied mob of rabid cats.

Spiros and Darda scrambled to their feet and hurried back to us. Tillit shouldered his cannon and grinned at the bedraggled pair. "Works every time."

Darda lunged at him with daggers drawn, but Spiros held her back.

"We do not have time to waste," Xander spoke up as he nodded at the top of the staircase.

The bats had made a path of tattered destruction. The subjects hung over the stair banister and were draped over the steps and ground. Black ink stained the floorboards and walls. The remaining bats flew up into the open rafters and nestled themselves in for a well-deserved rest, but they kept their eyes on the ink blood and squeaked as the black fluid shifted on the floor. The ooze slipped down the walls and across the boards to gather themselves at the pieces of fabric, coalescing into piles of cloth and ink that began to rise up and reform themselves.

"Hurry!" Xander ordered us as he grabbed my hand.

He whisked me down the hall and our friends followed close behind. Our feet clattered past the portrait creatures as they reached out their half-formed hands to snatch our ankles. We slipped past and turned a hard left into the throne room. The area was dark, but not quiet as we rushed inside and slammed the doors behind us. Spiros and Tillit shoved their shoulders against the entrances while Xander drew Darda and me deeper into the room.

A new noise joined the cacophony. This sound came from behind us. I spun around and noticed a figure draped over the chair. The shadow shifted and groaned again.

I grabbed Xander's arm and pointed at the figure. "Xander!" I whispered.

Xander drew his sword and pointed the blade at the stranger. He crept forward while Darda sidled up to me with a few daggers in each hand. A flash of lightning split the sky and illuminated the dark room, allowing us a chance at the groaning shadow.

I gasped. "Moneta!"

The figure was indeed our vanished hostess. She leaned over one of the arms of the chair with her back against the rear. Her head was tilted back and her mouth was open. Another groan escaped her parted lips.

At my exclamation Moneta stirred. Her eyes fluttered open and fell on our group. "What. . .what has happened?" Xander hurried to her side, but she held up a hand and stopped him. "I am fine."

"You are sure you are not injured?" he persisted.

She sat up and gave him a weak smile. "It would take far more than a blow to the head to destroy a goddess-" she winced and cupped her head, "-though they attempted to perform the job admirably."

DREAMS OF DRAGONS

"Who could have kidnapped you?" Xander asked her.

"Whoever it was doesn't happen to be really good at painting, do they?" I spoke up.

Tillit risked a glance over his shoulder at us. "Or be good at dropping a phantom into the house?"

Moneta started back. "You saw a phantom?"

I nodded. "Yeah, and it tried to convince us it was people we used to know."

"Then this creature recreated the faces of those long lost to you?"

"The voices, the faces, and a few portraits," I confirmed.

She tilted her head to one side and furrowed her brow. "Portraits?"

Tillit jerked his head toward the shut doors. "The subjects in your paintings decided they didn't want to sit still any longer so they climbed out and tried to get us."

She pursed her lips. "Then it must be the work of that demon."

"What demon?" Xander questioned her.

"The only demon-" Moneta tried to stand, but her legs wobbled beneath her. Xander caught her before she dropped back to the floor. She tilted her head up and looked into his face with shimmering tears in her eyes. "You must believe me when I say I am truly sorry for inviting your friends here."

"You were saying something about a demon," Tillit reminded her.

She hung her head as Xander helped her back onto her large chair where she slumped into its seat. Her voice sounded as exhausted as the storm outside was powerful. "Yes. There is a demon who has plagued me for many years. I believe it is he who haunts you now, for his dark powers are based on time."

"What sort of powers?" Spiros questioned her.

She raised her head and sighed. "Godly powers like mine for he is the last god on this plane aside from myself."

I started back. "And he's near here?"

Moneta nodded. "He is. Out there-" she pointed at the wall to her right, "-is another island larger than my own. On that island is the ruins of an ancient library, and within those ruins is a god who has stopped time to save his precious books." The last few words came out in a spat and her eyes hardened.

"An ancient-" My eyes widened. "You. . .you mean Crates?"

Moneta met my gaze with hers that were so full of anger. "I do."

Tillit folded his arms over his chest and snorted through his piggish nose. "Well, I guess that explains why he's been around for so long."

I shook my head. "But he gave us the chime. Why would he do that if he was a god?"

Moneta closed her eyes and a small chuckle escaped her lips. "Why would anyone wish to hand another the means of ridding himself of his only foes?"

"What power does he have over these phantoms?" Xander spoke up.

Our hostess opened her eyes and pursed her lips. "He is the god of time, and as such he can control the memories trapped within your minds." I noticed Tillit lifted his piggish nose and an eyebrow, but he said nothing.

"Why does he torment you and yours?" Darda asked her.

Moneta turned her face to the side and closed her eyes. "Once, long ago, he and I were lovers, but-" she grasped the fronts of the arms of the chair and furrowed her brow, "-there was a-well, a disagreement between us, and we chose different paths. I-" she waved a hand absently at the room, "-to my home and he to his library."

DREAMS OF DRAGONS

"You mentioned that the library lies in ruins. How did that come to be?" Xander wondered.

Moneta opened her eyes and glanced between Xander and myself. "You no doubt know Crates as a kind old man, but he is in fact very cunning and very ruthless. He sought to bring humans and naga-" she nodded at Xander, "-those from which your kind are descended. He desired to bring them all under his rule. I learned of his plans and created this storm which now surrounds us to lock him in." She hung her head and closed her eyes. "Unfortunately, in the creation of my storm I inadvertently destroyed the library and Crates within it."

"Can a god destroy another?" Darda asked her.

Moneta raised her head and a bitter laugh escaped her lips. "No, or we would have destroyed one another long ago. As it is he stopped time at the point where the library was destroyed."

I shook my head. "But I saw it. It isn't destroyed."

"What you witnessed was merely time suspended at the point of destruction," she told me. "Crates's powers gives him the ability to freeze time around himself."

Spiros furrowed his brow. "If he froze the library at the point of its destruction then how can there be ruins on the other island?"

"In freezing time he also captured the library in that moment, so as time moved on the library and himself remained in that point," she explained.

A heavy thud against the doors resounded through the throne room.

CHAPTER 17

We all stiffened. Tillit and Xander gripped their swords, Darda her daggers, and Tillit his strap. There came the pounding again.

"Is anyone in there?" The voice was that of Abraxas.

Tillit and Spiros glanced at each other. A smile slipped onto Spiros's lips. "The paintings have not yet talked."

Tillit shrugged and together they each grabbed a handle and pulled. The doors opened and revealed Abraxas flanked by several of his crewmen. His eyes fell on Moneta and widened. "My Lady!" He pushed past us and over to her where he knelt by her side.

Moneta cupped one of his cheeks in her palm and smiled down at him. "I am fine. The demon did me no harm."

"How did the 'demon' take you, anyway?" Tillit spoke up.

DREAMS OF DRAGONS

Moneta smiled and shook her head. "With Crates you can never tell how he works his powers. Perhaps he froze time for us and swept me away."

I glanced up at Xander. His lips were tightly pursed. "It *does* make sense."

He nodded. "Yes, but I do not know what steps might be taken-"

"I may be able to calm the storm enough to let you through to his island so that you might stop his ambitions forever," Moneta told us.

Xander arched an eyebrow. "So that we might send him away?"

She closed her eyes and bowed her head. "Yes. As you said of me, he is not welcome in this world. Allow me to help you on your mission."

"You'll be next," I reminded her.

Moneta raised her head and smiled. "I am aware of that, and after so many centuries guarding this world I am ready for my rest."

"My Lady, shall I remain with you?" Abraxas asked her.

She squeezed his hand and shook her head. "No. Lead them to the remains and help them end his foolish plans."

The captain nodded and rose to his feet before he turned to us. "Are you prepared?"

I crossed my arms over my chest and glared at him. "Who said we were going?"

"You must. My Lady has pleaded with you to finish this quarrel," he insisted.

"We will go," Xander announced.

I whipped my head up to him and frowned. "What are we going to do there? Knock on the front door and ask him to just let us chime him into his old world?"

"We will speak with him and see what we may discover," he told me before he turned to Abraxas. "Will we take our away boat?"

Abraxas nodded. "If you so choose, though there is a larger craft where my men and I will be able to row you much faster across the strait."

Tillit held up a finger. "We'll take that one, but could we hold off on the setting sail for just a few minutes? I need to speak to my compatriots about my sea-sickness."

Darda leaned back and frowned at him. "You do not have-"

"Among *other things*," he emphasized.

Xander turned to Abraxas. "We will join you at the docks in a few minutes."

Abraxas nodded. "Very well, though the dock for our boat is located on the western shore of this island in the direction of our destination."

"Is there a path to it?"

"Yes."

"Then we will have no trouble finding you," Xander assured him.

Abraxas bowed his head and hurried on his way. Tillit glanced at all of us and jerked his head toward the door. We followed him out into the corridor. The ghoulish paintings were gone, but the paper bats still clung to the rafters as testament to our last battle.

Tillit led us down the hall to the corner. A flash of lightning illuminated the area and revealed his tense expression. "I smell something rotten," he told us.

Darda turned up her nose. "It is no doubt the kitchen."

He shook his head. "Not literally. Over there-" he nodded in the direction we'd traveled. "I might not be able to get what everything that she was talking about, but Tillit does know when someone isn't telling the whole truth, and she wasn't."

DREAMS OF DRAGONS

Spiros glanced at Xander who stood beside him. "I, too, feel there is more than our hostess is telling."

Xander nodded. "That is possible-"

"Likely," Tillit corrected him.

"-but whatever secrets she holds will not be revealed until we have dealt with this new bit of information," Xander finished.

"So you really think she's telling the truth about Crates?" I asked him.

My dragon lord pursed his lips. "As Tillit mentioned, his being a god explains a great deal about the longevity of the library and him. However, we will ask him ourselves."

We proceeded downstairs, each with our own prioritized worries. My mind couldn't stay on one problem. The portrait fiends were gone but not forgotten, but Tillit's suspicions about our hostess bothered me. Then were was Crates. The revelations around him troubled me the most. I didn't like being lied to, particularly from a guy who'd sent us on two suicidal missions prior to this one only for us to find out he might've been the one to do it all himself if he'd taken the time to get his nose out of his precious books. Who better to deal with a god than a god? Or at least to give us a little bit of help other than enigmatic riddles.

We slipped out of the house, but our leaving didn't go unnoticed by the violent storm. Contrary to Moneta's promise the storm raged around us, battering us with hail and sleet. The wind nearly knocked me down, and it succeeded in knocking the breath out of me. Xander held tight to me while the others followed close behind as we made our way westward.

The land on that side was as barren as the rest of the island, but the rocks had been parted to create a narrow path that led down to the shore. A dock of some antiquity stretched from land out some forty feet into the water. A large away-boat waited for us, and at the oars were two of Abraxas's largest crew members. The captain himself knelt on the dock beside one of the anchor ropes that held the boat to the dock.

Without a word we piled inside and in two quick movements Abraxas had us untied. He leapt into the boat and the sturdy sailors rowed us away from the dock. Their oars cut through the rough waves like hot knives through butter, and no whitecap even slowed our pace. Tillit and Darda sat at the bow, Spiros at the rear with Abraxas, and I in a middle berth with Xander.

"How far is the island?" Xander asked Abraxas.

The captain gripped the handle of a rudder in one hand and guided us toward the dark point in the distance. "A mile, and my men will bring us there in less time than it takes to cut a sail."

Abraxas was true to his word, though I doubted if Moneta was. The storm never faltered as we rocked across the stormy seas to the other desolate island. At fifty yards I could see the island was as black as that of Moneta's, but flatter. A hulking mess of ruins sat in the center some quarter mile from the shoreline. The oarsmen drew us into a small cove where the burnt remains of a half dozen docks stood as silent sentinels to an ancient tragedy. The waves beat against their foundation pillars of stacked stone and wore them down with each successive century until only a few smoothed piles remained.

The sailors rowed within five feet of the shore and tucked in their oars before they leapt into the water. They drew us ashore and held the boat as we piled out onto the rocky soil. The wind blew into our faces, welcoming us to the island with a dry blast of wet ash. I shut my eyes and turned my face away to sputter the putrid dirt off my lips.

Xander slipped in front of me, protecting me from the harsh island. He glanced over his shoulder at the others, especially Abraxas who had joined us on the rock. "Where does Crates reside?"

DREAMS OF DRAGONS

Abraxas raised his hand and pointed a finger at the ruins. "There."

Darda shook her head. "But there is no library there."

"That was where the library stood, and where his powers keep it suspended in time," Abraxas told us.

"I don't care what was, is, or might be there," Tillit yelled above the wind. He wrapped his coat tighter around himself and buried his nose deep into the folds. His voice was muffled, but loud enough to hear. "Just get me out of this wind!"

Abraxas nodded. "Follow me."

The captain led us across the bleak terrain toward the ruins. I risked a glance at them and saw a few scorched walls and a doorway. The pair of wood doors, burned and cracked, had somehow survived the intense heat that brought down the grand building. The circular foundation showed its massive girth, and I didn't need the ruins to know its great height.

We reached the wreckage and stopped before the grand doors. Spiros glanced around. "Now what are we to do?"

Abraxas nodded at the doors. "If Crates wishes to see you then you need merely enter."

A knocker, the head of a griffin, hung from one of the entrances. I reached up and brushed my hand against the familiar face. We all started back as the door creaked open. Xander drew me behind him and unsheathed his sword before he opened the door with the tip of his weapon. The entrance opened and revealed the bleak interior of the ruins.

I pursed my lips as another blast of cold wind hit me. "Great. He probably knows why we're here and won't talk to-" I paused. Movement from beyond the doorway had caught my attention. The air appeared to shimmer like the rippling surface of water.

"Miriam?" Xander asked me.

I furrowed my brow and shook my head as I took a step closer to the open door. "I don't know." I raised my arm and my fingertips teased the threshold. "There's just-" An invisible forced wrapped around my wrist and yanked me through the doorway.

"Miriam!" I heard my friends yell behind me as I toppled onto the ground.

I expected a puff of blackened dirt to greet me, but I found myself on smooth, polished stone. The light around me changed from dreary black to a soft warm glow. I raised my head and found myself staring at the center of the library not more than twenty feet from me. Gone was the desolate ruins, and instead all around me were the smooth walls of the ancient center of learning. The candles were lit around the center area, but not down the wide corridor in which I found myself.

I started when a hand settled on my shoulder. Xander knelt beside me with his sword in his other hand. A creak warned us of danger, and I looked over my shoulder in time to watch the door slam into Darda's face, shoving her outside and into the unprepared arms of Spiros and Tillit. Xander rushed the closing portal, but the door shut with such a force that its frame rattled. He grabbed the handle and pulled. The door didn't budge.

I scrambled to my feet and joined him at the door. My efforts proved to be just as futile.

"Let me try again," Xander offered as he handed me Bucephalus. He grabbed the handle with both hands and yanked. The door didn't budge. He straightened and shook his head. "We shall not escape through there."

That meant Xander and I were trapped alone in the den of the beast.

DREAMS OF DRAGONS

CHAPTER 18

A flickering light appeared behind us. I turned and watched as the candles along the walls on either side of us were lit by invisible hands. The trail of illumination traveled to the center of the library and around the balconies, giving us a look at the familiar countless rows of books that stretched up and down the many levels of the majestic Mallus Library.

A figure draped in shadows stood before the railing that surrounded the center of the library. Their hands were clasped behind their back and their glowing yellow eyes were glued to us.

I tapped on Xander's shoulder. "Um, Xander?"

Xander turned. His eyes fell on the figure and his hand moved to grasp the hilt of the sword clasped between my shaking hands.

"There is no need for that, King of Alexandria," Crates called to us.

Xander narrowed his eyes at our friend turned possible foe. "Are these words as deceitful as those in times past?"

Crates stepped into the full light of the candles. His eyes resumed their normal dark color, and in the glow of the candles I could see his face was long and tired. For the first time I had a glimpse of his true age, a life of countless years that stretched into millennia.

Crates sighed. "I am truly sorry that I hid the full truth from you."

My eyes widened and my lips parted. "Then you. . .you really are the last god, aren't you?"

He bowed his head. "Yes. I am the god of time, and all the knowledge time grants. I know what was, what is, and what will be."

"Why did you not tell us sooner?" Xander questioned him.

Crates pursed his lips and turned away so his back faced us. He bowed his head and when he spoke his voice was very quiet. "I, too, did not wish to leave this wondrous world, but I better than anyone understood the effects my kin and I were having on the world." He glanced over his shoulder and smiled at us. "That is why I entrusted the task of finding my siblings to you."

"And why you couldn't ring the bell yourself," I surmised.

He half-turned to us and nodded. "Yes."

Xander slipped between Crates and me, and glared at our deceptive friend. "Then was it a lie that the other gods were a danger to our world? Did you not wish for them to be removed so you might take this world as your own?"

Crates met Xander's gaze with a steady one. "You yourself witnessed the awesome power my brethren held. Do you believe they were a blessing to this fragile world?"

Xander shook his head. "No, but why did you not offer yourself as the first to be banished?"

DREAMS OF DRAGONS

"I chose to remain to be your guide, though soon even that little duty will be lost to me," Crates told us. His eyes flickered between us and his face fell. "I see I have not convinced you of my sincerity. Moneta's poisonous words run too deep."

"Even if she isn't telling the truth *you* were the first one to deceive us," I reminded him.

He closed his eyes and gave a nod. "Yes, and for that I deserve your mistrust. However-" he opened his eyes and took a step backward, "-I must ask for your faith again. You must rid this world of Moneta before I am banished. She is more dangerous than you can imagine, and a far worse foe than any you have ever faced."

Xander took Bucephalus from me and pointed the sword at the god. "We will send her from this world, but after we have removed you from it, as well."

Crates shook his head. "That cannot be done. Your world would be doomed."

"An hour between sendings will be all the difference for you two," Xander promised.

A sly smile slipped onto the old man's wrinkled lips. "I am afraid I will not be able to cooperate, but I wish you good luck in sending Moneta."

A shadow and a screech from above us made me look up. The griffin crashed into the floor between Crates and us. Its claws dug deep into the wood and blasted dust and splinters in all directions. Xander drew me back and held Bucephalus up in front of him. The blessed sword glowed against the snapping beak of the beast.

The griffin took a few steps toward us, forcing us backwards. Xander swung his sword and clipped the creature's beak. The beast reared back its head and loosed a roar that echoed over the library. The noise reverberated through my eardrums and head, causing a terrible, pain-filled tremor in my mind. I clapped my hands over my ears and scrunched my eyes shut.

Xander's strong arms wrapped around me and he nearly carried me toward the exit. I opened my eyes in time to watch him fling open one of the doors. The handle gave way without protest and he half-dragged me across the threshold. Xander stumbled over the uneven ground as smooth stone changed to blackened rock.

The doors slammed shut behind us, but the force was too much for the aged wood. The doors shattered and cracked. One fell askew on its hinges and the other fell to the ground in several pieces. The special gateway beyond the threshold was now lost to time.

Darda wrapped her arms around me tighter than a grizzly. "Miriam! Oh Miriam, what happened? Are you hurt?"

I dropped my hands from my ears and returned her hug. "I'm fine, just a little vibrated."

Spiros set his hand on Xander's tense shoulder and looked over his old friend. "What happened?"

"We were kicked out," I told him.

Tillit snorted. "A fine way to treat guests."

Xander turned to Abraxas who watched us with careful eyes. "We must return to your mistress and inform her that the gate is closed to the library. Perhaps she may know of another way into Crates's domain."

The captain pursed his lips, but nodded. We were led back to the boat. The oarsmen had dragged part of the boat on shore. We piled into the vessel and pushed off for the far island. The storm picked up in intensity, creating huge waves out the whitecaps. The boat rocked to and fro amid the anger of the storm. We climbed tall hills of waves only to crash down onto the foothills of another one.

Tillit grasped the side of the boat as a wave hit the other side, nearly toppling us. "If this is her idea of lessening the storm than I'd hate to make her mad!"

DREAMS OF DRAGONS

Abraxas's gaze was glued to the far island. His expression was one of tension, but there was an empty look in his eyes. "My Lady is already mad."

I looked past Xander at our helmsman. "What do you mean by that?"

Abraxas let slip his hand from the rudder and stood. Spiros was quick to take command of the boat, but that mattered little as our oarsmen tossed their oars into the stormy seas and also rose to their feet. Xander and Tillit made grabs for the planks, but the heavy wood was quick to sink beneath the tumbling surface.

Abraxas's cold, distant voice cut through the wild winds and sea-spray as his attention lay fixed on the island. "She demands we return without you. May you find peace among these stormy waves."

The three men jumped overboard and disappeared into the raging strait. Darda let out a strangled scream that was swallowed by a clap of thunder. Spiros held the rudder handle with both hands, but without the oarsmen we were shoved about like a cork.

Tillit was shoved against the side. His hands grasped the edges to keep him from going over before he whipped his head over his shoulder at me. "A little help, Neito Vedesta!"

I shook off the shock of what had just happened and scurried over to the side. Xander wrapped his arms around my waist and kept me in the boat as I leaned over and stretched my arms over the violent waves. I shut my eyes and furrowed my brow as I focused all my thoughts on the unruly waters beneath our tiny vessel.

The water bubbled under us and with a splash of spray two large dragons burst from the ocean. Their lithe bodies raised up our boat from the homicidal water, though the waves still splashed at us as though grasping for its lost prey. My dragons let out long, soothing calls before they cut through the stormy seas toward the foreboding house on the desolate hill.

Tillit clutched his strap with one hand and the boat with the other as we shot through the water. "You think it was something we said that got her so riled?"

Xander drew me back into the boat while I kept my hands raised and my focus on my dragons. His attention settled on the dark shadow of the house that loomed before us. "I believe your suspicions about her truthfulness are well-founded."

A large wave tried to upset us from the backs of my wet steeds, but one of the beasts cut the wild water in two and we were merely sprayed. Tillit winced. "For once I wish I wasn't always so right and ruggedly handsome."

Darda rolled her eyes. "How can you make such foolish jokes when our lives are in danger?"

He shrugged. "It keeps me from reminding myself that none of us has any plan on how to sneak up on a goddess who's entrenched herself on her own private island with a bunch of sailors who aren't going to be too happy to learn that they're captain and shipmates committed suicide because we failed to convince a god to go home."

Spiros glanced to our right and his eyes widened. "I do not believe we will have to worry about the ire of the sailors."

We followed his gaze and glimpsed a shadow looming up in the storm. The many masts and pale crew told all of us it was the Acheron. Her sails were open wide and she flew across the waves like a ship possessed. The thought occurred to me that maybe it was when I glimpsed the unmistakable figure at the helm.

It was Abraxas, alive and steering the bow of the ship straight at our little vessel.

DREAMS OF DRAGONS

CHAPTER 19

Darda's mouth dropped open. "But how is this possible?" She turned to us and shook her head. "He...did he not drown?"

Xander pursed his lips as he studied our incoming foe. "Perhaps the sailors of Alexandria are more than they appear."

"Or less," Spiros mused.

My eyebrows crashed down as I raised my hands. "Either way we're getting out of here."

My water dragons turned to the left so that our bow pointed toward the rear of the island. The ghostly vessel turned slightly, intent on intercepting us. I clenched my teeth and willed my dragons on as quickly as I could, but the storm blew against us and slowed our escape. For the grand ship the wind filled its sails and hurried her along to our impending doom.

"They intend to ram us!" Darda yelped.

"Brace for impact!" Xander shouted.

Everyone clung to the boat as my dragons craned their necks to escape the oncoming vessel. The Acheron was fifty-no, forty-feet away and closing. I tensed as I prepared for the inevitable.

A second large shadow emerged from the messy seas. Its bow pointed at that of the Acheron and the ghostly ship, intent on clashing with us, was unaware of the second vessel until it was too late to turn. The bows collided in a grinding of wood and steel nails. Their masts crashed into one another, and rigging and sails joined into impossible knots. Splinters flew everywhere and the force of the collision threw the Acheron off course. The vessel missed us by ten feet, slicing the waves at our stern. We had a front-row seat to the bow of the attacking ship.

"The Blå Engel!" Darda yelled.

Our savior was indeed Magnus's ship. The vessel wasn't dead in the water, but she was locked in too tightly to escape the crash without some effort. Unfortunately, the crew of the Acheron had every intention of revenging themselves on the interfering ship. The ghostly crew swung from the ropes and jumped the narrow gap between the vessels, and a small war erupted on the deck of the Blå Engel.

Spiros whipped his head to Xander. "We must help them!"

I clenched my teeth and drew my dragons in a tight turn. The effort nearly tore the boat apart as we slammed through several towering waves to get at our nautical friends. My dragons raised our boat above the railing and we were deposited with a crash onto the deck. Several of the invaders were trapped beneath the boat, and both sides gawked at our arrival.

We were equally shocked by what we saw. The sailors of the Acheron had gotten the worst of Magnus's crew. Some of their limbs lay limp on the deck, but the appendages flopped around like they were still attached. The stump on the sailors' bodies revealed rotten pieces of flesh beneath their tanned exterior. No blood poured out, and they showed no signs of pain as they resumed their attack on the ship.

"By all the gods. . ." Darda whispered.

"We cannot rely on them," Xander quipped as he drew his sword.

Spiros and Xander leapt from the boat with swords drawn and joined the fray. Darda sliced her way toward the bow while Tillit sidled up to me. His eyes flickered to me and he gave me a wink. "I think this deck could use a little bit of sea scrubbing, don't you?"

I grinned and nodded. "I think it could."

I stood in our little stranded boat and put two fingers to my mouth. My whistle blew across the deck and over the wide seas. The crashing waves bubbled, and from the depths came dozens of my smaller dragons, thin and long like snakes. They rose up equal to the sails on the open side of the Blå Engel before they rushed the deck. Their slim bodies flew past our friends, but wrapped around our foes. They dragged the Alexandrian guard off the deck and into the gap between vessels. Their cries were interrupted with a splash as they disappeared into the sloshing waves. Others were dropped onto their own deck while my dragons turned sharply upward into the messy sails.

They stopped at the ropes and knots and, with their long jaws, worked away at the bound material until the masts were freed from one another. My dragons used their heads to push the ships apart and I gave a wave to the savage crew of the Acheron as we parted ways. I had my powers shove the other ship far out into the white waves while we ourselves were pushed closer to the island.

At the end of the separation my dragons disappeared, and so did my strength. I collapsed onto my knees and clutched my head in one hand. Tillit knelt beside me and held my shoulders as Xander and the others hurried up to me.

My dragon lord knelt in front of me and cupped one of my cheeks in his hand. He raised my eyes and he searched my face with anxious eyes. "You did not need to push yourself so hard."

I gave him a weak smile. "I couldn't let you guys have all the fun."

A pair of boots clumped across the deck and I looked to my left to find the pair of captains, Magnus and Alice, standing over our group. The captain grinned at me. "Not a bad way of cleaning the deck, My Lady. Ah'll have ta give ya ship duties later."

Alice glared at him. "If there is a later." She turned her attention to Xander. "Why did the crew of the Acheron want to ram your ship?"

"We disappointed their mistress and she wants us out of the way now," Tillit spoke up.

Magnus arched an eyebrow. "Disappointed how?"

Xander stood and shook his head. "The tale is too long to tell." He pointed at the foreboding structure that loomed ahead of us. A chill went down my spine as my gaze fell on the dark windows, like empty eyes wanting to swallow us, body and soul. "At the moment we must reach the house and banish her from this world."

"Captain!" the sailor at the helm called to us.

I couldn't help but notice it wasn't Nimeni. A quick sweep of the deck showed he wasn't there, either. "Where's Nimeni?" I asked the captain.

"Still resting," Magnus replied as he hurried to the bottom of the stairs that led up to the wheel. "What is it?"

The sailor pointed at the starboard side where a great shadow hurried through the waves toward us. "She's coming, and quick!"

Magnus whipped his head back to look up into the mess of ropes. Many of them hung down with one end dangling over the deck. A few of the sails sported tears that the men were trying to sew up with large needles made of bone and wood. "Open the sails!"

One of the men handling the center sail glanced down and shook his head. "They're open as much as they can be without tearing them apart!"

"Damn it!" Magnus swore.

"For the love of the sea!" Alice snapped as she pushed him aside and looked up at the sailors. "Use your heads, you dolts, and use your wings as sails! Or use them to cover the patches in the sails!"

The men looked to their captain, who glared at them and waved a hand at the sails. "Well? What are ya waiting for? That ship to catch us?" His sailors nodded and hurried to heed Alice's advice. Magnus turned to Alice and grinned. "Ah knew Ah hadn't married ya for yer beauty alone."

"Compliments *after* we've reached shore," Tillit advised them.

The ship, under the renewed power of its sailors, leapt forward over the waves and sped toward the westward side of the island. Xander wrapped his arms around me and pressed me close to his chest.

I looked up at him and frowned. His face was tense and his eyes remained on the house. "What are you doing?"

"The ship cannot land," he reminded me as I felt his body tense. "Therefore, we must fly the remaining distance to the island."

My eyes widened and my mouth dropped open. "Fly? In this wind? Hell no." I squirmed in his hold. "Just let me get out my dragons and-"

"No." His voice was firm and uncompromising. I looked into his face and he met my gaze with his steady one. "You have used a great deal of your strength to help us. Now I will use mine to help you."

I rolled my eyes, but a smile teased my lips. "All right, you can be a hero, too, but don't do anything stupid."

Spiros strode over to the starboard railing and grasped the wood. He leaned out over the waves and squinted at the oncoming vessel. "I believe our foes have already begun such an act."

We looked where his eyes lay and watched as half the crew of the Acheron took flight from the deck and rigging. The cruel winds of the storm died down around them so that they were able to fly directly at us without a breath of trouble.

Tillit stepped up to Spiros's side and pursed his lips. "I don't think flying's such a good idea anymore."

Spiros slipped behind the sus and hooked his arms under our portly friend as a mischievous smile danced across his lips. "Nonsense. This will only make it more exciting."

"Exciting?" Tillit yelped as he tried to free himself from Spiros's hold. "Dying is not exciting!"

"We will do no such thing," Darda scolded him as she spread her dragon wings out behind her. "Not so long as we have such an important task at hand."

"But-hey!" Spiros spread his wings and flapped into the air. The sus kicked his feet, but they touched nothing except air as Spiros flew them over the railing.

Xander lifted me into his arms and followed them, as did Darda. The angered winds blew against us, nearly toppling us into the savage sea below. Half of the sailors from the Acheron came to a stop in front of us and the other half, including the mysteriously alive Abraxas, flew on to the house where they landed.

I wished we could've done the same as thunder shook the air around us. Instead, a wall of hostile dragons hovered in our way. That is, until loud cannon fire at our backs sounded our victory knell. What flew past us wasn't the balls of hard shot but round paper balls. The balls were a little off course because of the wind, but they came close enough to

DREAMS OF DRAGONS

the wall of dragons that the sailors flew to meet them. The sailors drew out their short swords and cut the balls open, unleashing what lay inside.

Black water poured out of the balls, and out of that black water sprung a small shape with eight legs. The limbs wrapped around the attacking dragons and dragged them down into the thrashing waves.

Tillit whooped. "Go, mathair shuigh!"

I blinked at him. "What are those things?"

"Mathair shuigh are small squids native to Cayden's region," Xander told me with a smile on his face. "They are very aggressive when attacked, and are known to drag their enemies into the water to drown them."

My eyes widened. "And Magnus had *those* on board?"

Tillit glanced at me and grinned. "They were in the crates he kept aboard. A neat trick to put them in the cannons, wasn't it?"

"We must hurry while they are distracted!" Darda reminded us.

Half the dragons were in the water, leaving gaping holes in the defenses in front of us. Spiros, Xander and Darda pumped their wings and flew between the gaps. The sailors gave chase, but we reached the top of the island before them and raced inside.

We found an unwelcome group waiting for us.

CHAPTER 20

The large foyer was lit with candles and the many flashes of lightning. The area was also filled with the sailors of the Acheron and their captain. They stood before the grand staircase, and a few steps up was our objective, Moneta. She stood tall with a coy smile on her lips.

"Welcome back, my dear friends," she cooed as the sailors swung around to surround us on all sides. The doors were shut behind us, trapping us in with the unwelcome-wagon.

I snorted. "Yeah, we're friends because friends try to get friends to do their dirty work."

She laughed as she walked down the stairs and draped her withered arms over Abraxas's shoulders. "I would gladly have done Crates in long ago, but you see-" her eyes fell on the backpack on my back, "-without that chime it is impossible for a god to truly defeat another god."

DREAMS OF DRAGONS

"You sought to use us as you accused Crates of using us," Xander accused her.

Moneta bowed her head. "Yes, and I thought after your defeating of my other siblings that the job would have been easy for you. You have no idea how disappointed I was when my toy-" she curled her fingers through Abraxas's hair, "-told me you had failed."

Spiros's eyes flickered to the silent captain. The expressions on Abraxas and his men were blank, and their eyes were devoid of recognition. "Are these truly the sailors of Alexandria?"

Moneta nodded. "Oh yes. These poor men were lost at sea in my storm. I thought they might come in useful as scouts, so I dredged up their memories from the bottom of the ocean and put them to work in my service."

Darda's mouth dropped open. "Such sacrilege! The dead deserve to rest!"

The goddess laughed and shook her head. "Even I do not have the power to revive the dead. No, these little boys-" she rubbed her cheek against that of Abraxas, "-are merely memories of their former selves. Shades, if you will, made solid by my powers."

"And completely in your power," Xander surmised.

"Yes. They would 'die' for me, if that is what I wished, though truly they cannot die so long as I reside in this world," she mused.

"Why do you use them as your scouts? Why have you resided on this island in this house for so long? For what did you wait?" Spiros questioned her.

A flash of lightning struck my womanly intuition. My eyes widened and my lips parted. A single whispered words passed my lips. "Crates. . ."

A flash of anger swept over her features, marring her beauty for a second before a smile made the look flee. "Yes. Dear Crates. Dear, dear-" Her chuckle interrupted her own words. The storm outside picked up. Its winds slammed against the house, rattling the very timbers. She swept a hand through her hair and shook her head, and the wind calmed a little. "He knew how I felt, and yet he chose you-" her narrowed eyes swept over us, "-you *mortals*. He chose to store your knowledge in that *stupid* library and ignore me. Ignore this-" she gestured to the house around us. A bitter laugh escaped her lips and was punctuated by a crash of thunder. "I took this house from those who built it, those filthy nagas who thought themselves too good to give this wonderful house to a god. So I destroyed them and took it for us, but Crates-" she hung her head. "He thought my taking their lives was a terrible sin, as though a god could sin, so he locked himself in his library." She leaned her head back and smiled, but her eyes were filled with tears. "I realized then that he wouldn't love me, so a single lightning strike on a few bits of brush. The entire island was aflame in a few minutes." She draped herself over Abraxas again and lay her chin on his shoulder as she smiled at us. "I watched the flames eat at the foundation, and then-" her mood changed. Her eyes narrowed and a flash of lightning illuminated the shadows on her face. "-then the library flickered for a moment-a brief moment-and though the flames consumed the structure I knew-" She dropped off Abraxas and slipped between him to stand between us and the mob. "-I knew he had used his powers to freeze the library in time, a place where memories resided but where I could not go."

"I'm going to guess that you're the god of memories," Tillit spoke up.

Moneta bowed her head. "I am, and soon that will be all you are." She glanced over her shoulder at Abraxas. "Deal with them."

The captain and his crew drew out their long swords and short daggers, and stalked toward us. My friends and I made a circle and stepped backwards so that our backs were pressed together.

DREAMS OF DRAGONS

Tillit looked over his shoulder at us. "Does anyone happen to have a good idea?"

Darda glared at him. "*You* are the one with the satchel of endless trouble."

He glanced back at our enclosing foes and shook his head. "I don't think I've got time to find it."

She arched an eyebrow. "Do you truly have something in mind?"

The sus nodded as the tips of the sailors swords came within inches of our throats. "I think I do."

A sly smile slipped onto my lips as I balled my hands into fists at my sides. A little bit of water leaked out of them and onto the floor. "I hope you don't mind my poking my nose into your conversation, but I think I might have something to help you."

Moneta's eyes widened as she noticed the puddles that appeared beneath my fists. She stabbed a finger at us. "Kill them!"

The sailors lunged at us, but I had enough time to throw up my arms. A wall of water rose up around us, protecting us in a cylinder of wetness. The sailors hesitated at the threshold, but Abraxas drew back his weapon and stabbed at the wall. His weapon went through the water and nearly struck Spiros in the thigh had he not twisted aside.

Tillit grabbed Darda's shoulder and shoved her down to the floor. "Let's keep our heads about us, shall we?"

She grabbed the strap of his satchel and gave a tug. "Then make use of yours and start digging!"

Tillit grinned and slapped down his bag. He began rummaging as our fight began. The sailors tested the waters with more daggers. I raised my hands. Small dragons stretched out from the wall and wrapped their lithe bodies around the weapons. With a quick yank most of them were disarmed, but some of them were prepared with backups and those that kept hold of their weapons leapt back. A half dozen of the sailors drew out daggers from beneath their white sailor coats and threw them at us.

Xander drew me down and Spiros joined us on the floor. The sudden change in altitude meant my concentration was broken, and so was the wall. The water flickered and dropped in half so that if we stood our upper half would be revealed.

"Ah-ha!" Tillit shouted as he drew out a slingshot and a small leather pouch. "This should do the trick!"

Darda's mouth dropped open. "You must be joking! That is what will save us?"

"Just you watch!" Tillit told her as he dug into the bag. He drew out a small bit of round shot, loaded the sling of the slingshot, and leapt to his feet. The presentation of a sus holding a slingshot dumbfounded our foes, giving Tillit time to aim at the thickest bunch of sailors. "This might sting a little."

Tillit fired off the shot. The ball flew at the sailors and landed at their feet. The wall behind them blew apart inwardly, sending them face-planting onto the floor. Debris carpeted the room, sending all of us ducking for cover. After the dust settled we raised our heads and saw there was a gaping hole in the front of the house. Half-blown boards hung askew and we could see the interior of the structure.

The truth of the house was revealed by the hole, and the dilapidated look Xander and I had seen was on full display between the walls. The boards were rotten and filled with squirming maggots. Water dripped from the wallpaper and onto the molding floor where a wide assortment of ferns grew to the sub-flooring of the second story.

Darda's eyes widened before she looked to the sus. "What is in those balls?"

Tillit blinked as he looked from the massive hole in the wall to the slingshot in his hand. "I guess this thing packs a bigger punch than I remember."

DREAMS OF DRAGONS

A figure stepped into the gaping hole, tall and proud. At their hip was a gleaming sword and in their eyes was a wild glint.

I blinked at the familiar face. "Alice?"

"And Ah'm here," Magnus spoke up as he appeared at her side. In one hand he held the neck of one of the sailors. He tossed the unconscious man to the rubbled-filled floor and spat at him. "Damned if these things aren't stubborn."

"Destroy all of them!" Moneta commanded her men.

Magnus puffed out his belly and grinned. "Not likely." More figures appeared behind them, the whole of his crew. They brandished their swords and in their eyes was a glint as mad as that of Alice. Magnus nodded at the former sailors in front of him. "Get 'em."

A collision of good and evil took place in that foyer which had suddenly become too small. Swords clashed and men flew everywhere. My friends joined in the fray with their weapons as I wrapped my water dragons around our foes and tossed them about the room.

The skirmish eased toward the stairs. I watched Moneta rushed up the stairs with the energy of someone half her age and disappeared into her throne room. I dropped the pack onto the ground and pulled the chime box out. Frantic footsteps made me look up. One of the sailors rushed at me with arms outstretched and a look of fury on his face.

Tillit swooped in from the crowd of fighters and body-slammed into the man's side. The sailor careened into the wall and slumped down to the floor. He turned to me with a grin and a wink. "Don't worry about nothing, Miriam. Tillit has-" Another sailor came up behind him and threw a punch that hit Tillit square in the back of the head. The sus stumbled forward and fell onto his knees.

I raised my hand to help, but a dagger flew through the air and captured the man's large cuffs. The velocity of the weapon yanked him backward and he fell onto his back beside Tillit. Tillit leaned over and slammed his fist into the sailor's nose. The appendage popped off and bounced across the floor.

Tillit leaned back and wrinkled his piggish nose. "These guys have seen better days."

"Stop talking and keep fighting!" Darda scolded him as she strode up to my side and helped me to my feet. Her dress was cut open and revealed a black body suit beneath with a waistband full of daggers. Many of the slots were already empty. She gave me a gentle push toward the stairs. "Hurry on and send that goddess back to her world!"

I nodded and rushed up the stairs. The doors to the throne room were shut, but unlocked. I rushed through them and found myself in the dark room. The doors slammed shut behind me and a flash of lightning added to the effect. The bolt illuminated the dirty windows and the decrepit room. Gone was the facade of upkeep, and in its place was the shambles of a once-proud room.

Moneta sat in her chair with her slender arms draped over the arms of the furniture. A sly, crooked smile graced her lips. She raised one hand and beckoned to me with her fingers. "Come to me, my little toy. Come to sweet memory."

The air around her flickered. Her form shivered like a ripple across water. I blinked, and Moneta was gone. In her place sat my father, his arms held out to me. There was a smile on his face.

I narrowed my eyes and held out the chime. "You tried that trick already, remember?"

I blinked again, and my father vanished. Moneta sat in her chair with her smile, but there was a touch of anger in its corners. "Perhaps I have, but have you seen this one?"

She raised her hand and snapped her fingers, and it was as though a cloak fell from her body. Countless decades fell away and revealed a beautiful woman of thirty with shimmering black hair and smooth skin. She now wore a slim-fitting red dress that showed off her legs that went all the way up.

Moneta crossed those smooth, elegant legs and laid her arms on the chair. "Surely you didn't believe a goddess would let herself become a crippled old woman, do you?"

I tightened my trembling fingers around the handle of the bell as I glared at her. "Only an honest one."

She chuckled. "In all my many years I have learned that honesty doesn't win."

"Neither will you," I argued as I took a step toward her.

She snapped her fingers again. The floor gave way beneath me and I dropped into a dark, square pit some twenty feet deep. The bottom was filled with six feet of water so that I was dunked, but I could push off from the bottom. I broke through the surface with the bell still clenched in my hand and looked up. The walls were of ancient brick and on all sides four feet above me were wide, sloped holes.

The square light above me was blotted out by the appearance of Moneta. She knelt beside the hole and leaned over. "You may be able to swim, my dear, but can you do when the water won't obey you?"

A rumbling noise alerted me to danger a half second before a deluge of water flowed out of the holes. The hundreds of gallons spilled down on me with all the wrath of its beckoning mistress. I was shoved beneath the cold waves and slammed against the floor. Even with my unique senses I couldn't tell up from down inside the swirling mess of bubbles and spilling water.

There was only one way to get out of this tempest in a pit. I closed my eyes and activated my water sense.

I gasped and bubbled floated up as my mind was bombarded with a million different stories being played out in the water. Too late did I realize that the water spilling into my pit was from the ocean. My mind was captured by the countless stories and shoved into the oblivion of unconsciousness.

DREAMS OF DRAGONS

CHAPTER 21

"Miriam!"

My eyes flew open and all my instincts told me to swim. There was nothing to paddle through for my arms, but my feet kicked off the cheap commercial carpet and pushed my chair forward. One of my paddling hands got caught between the chair and the desk in front of me, and pain shot up my arm as the fingers were pinched by my weight.

I yelped and tugged my fingers out of the pincer attack of my own making. A laugh made me look up. My old friend Heather stood over me, and behind her leaning against the doorway of the cubicle was Blake, the sus who'd kidnapped me all those many months ago. He was his cute human self now.

My mischievous human friend set her hands on her knees and leaned down so we were eye-level. "You want me to kiss it and make it all better?"

"Wha-?" I muttered.

My eyes blinked a lot as they took in the view around me. I sat at my computer desk in my old cubicle. The familiar scent of sweating coworkers and stale coffee invaded my nostrils. Feet shuffled down the narrow aisles between the cubicles and a constant hum of computers and murmur of people exercised my ears.

I looked up at Heather. "How'd I get here?"

"You drove," she told me.

I shook my head. "Not here, *here*. You know, in this world."

It was her turn to blink. "What are you talking about?"

I grabbed her hand and looked her in the eyes. "What am I talking about? You remember Xander! I told you about me falling in love with that dragon lord and you helped me get back through the portal to our-his world!"

She shook her head. "I don't know what you're talking about, but if you've got one of those guys hidden in your closet then you'd better share."

Blake came over and set a hand on my shoulder. He looked down at me and studied me with pursed lips. "Are you feeling okay, Miriam?"

I shrugged off his hand and glared at him. "Of course I'm okay! I just want to know what the hell is going on and why the hell you're back in this world!"

Heather slipped between the desk and my chair and clapped a hand over my mouth. "Not so loud!"

"You're making a scene, that's what's going on," Blake warned me as he peered over the top of the cubicle at the rest of the office floor. "And people are starting to notice."

I tore Heather's hand off my mouth and glared up at her. "Will you please tell me what's going on?"

Heather stood on her tiptoes and peeked over the top. She winced. "Trouble, that's what."

DREAMS OF DRAGONS

I stood and followed her gaze. A half dozen people stared over the walls of my cubicle. There were also a few peekers from the offices around the external walls.

I plopped myself back into my chair and ran a hand through my hair. "I don't get it. One minute I was drowning and the next I'm here."

Heather frowned down at me. "Drowning? That nightmare again?"

I dropped my hand and arched an eyebrow at my friend. "What nightmare?"

"You have nightmares about water," Blake reminded me.

Heather folded her arms across her chest and nodded. "Yeah, and about being eating my huge dragons. You've been having them for a couple of weeks now."

I slumped back in my chair and focused my sight on the ragged carpet as I furrowed my brow. "Nightmares?"

"We wanted to take you to a psychiatrist so he could analyze your dreams, but you've been insisting that you're fine," Blake added.

"Dreams. . ." I whispered. I sat up and shook my head. "It. . .it can't be. All that stuff I went through couldn't have been a dream."

Heather knelt down in front of me and caught my gaze in her own. "You didn't go through anything except some really bad dreams."

Blake set a hand on my shoulder and smiled down at me. "How about we go get that lunch? My treat."

Heather frowned at him. "You said I had to pay today or we'd all starve."

He shrugged. "Today's an exception, especially with Miriam not feeling well." He returned his attention to me and slipped a gentle hand beneath one of my arms. "Hurry it up before the lunch hour is over and we really *are* all forced to starve."

"Or sneak food in via our pants," Heather suggested.

Blake cringed and his hand on my arm became more insistent. "I'd rather not."

Heather laughed and slapped his back, nearly knocking him over. "Then get going!" A ghost of a smile slipped onto my lips as Heather took my arm and tugged me out of my cubicle and into the nearest elevator. Blake had a hard time keeping up with us as the doors opened to the lobby and my friend dragged me through the familiar front doors to the busy street beyond "Women and children first!"

Miriam.

I paused and whipped my head around. That voice sounded familiar, but there weren't any other familiar faces on the street other than those of my companions. My friends stopped a few steps ahead and turned back to me.

Heather jerked her head in the direction ahead of them. "Come on! Last one there picks up the tab!"

"I already said I was going to pick up the tab," Blake reminded her.

"We're moving the goal posts!" she announced as she slipped up to my side and looped one of her arms through mine. "Now come on!"

Heather half dragged me to the diner on the corner which had been a hangout for my friends for a long time. It had been so long since I'd been in there, but the smells and sights were still familiar. Or had it?

Had all of those adventures been a dream? A feverish figment of my overactive imagination? Was I really back here in this doldrum job with my silly friend at my side and the non-malevolent Blake as a cute tag-along?

I took a seat in a corner booth with Heather pinning me between her body and the wall, and Blake opposite us. The scent of cigarette smoke lingered in the upholstery and more than one office slave was partaking in an early nightcap. We ordered our food, the delicious, greasy meals for which the diner was famous. Everything tasted as I remembered it. Everything was like it was in those halcyon days of innocence. And yet, at the back of my mind I felt something wasn't quite right.

That feeling stayed with me for the rest of the day. At the end of work Heather and I walked together through the lobby and out into the cool night air. She wrapped her coat closer and turned to me with a grin and a wink. "Want to go out on the town? My treat."

I shook my head. "N-no, I think I'll just go home."

Heather's face fell and her lips turned into a pout. "Ah, come on, the night is young and so are we. It's the perfect combination."

I took a step back and gave her a wave. "I'll see you tomorrow, Heth." I turned and walked down the street to the parking garage.

"Not if I'm still drunk!" Heather shouted.

I rolled my eyes, but kept walking. The night air refreshed me a little, and I found myself humming a little tune as I reached my car. I reached out with the key in my hand to unlock the door.

Miriam.

My head whipped up and I spun around. A few other stragglers were in the garage, but none of them paid the slightest attention to me. I took a step back from the car and looked in through the windows. The backseat was empty, and so were the floorboards across the entire car.

I clutched my chest and took a deep breath. It was just my imagination. Maybe the grease from the diner was getting to me.

But you heard the sound before that.

"Shut up. . ." I muttered to myself as I slipped into the car.

I drove to my apartment, that refreshing little hole that hinted at long-ago cigarettes and tawdry rendezvous. The same old peeling wallpaper. The same old scuffed floorboards. Everything was just as I remembered it.

"Makes me miss the castle," I mused as I set my purse on the table beside the door. I paused and shook my head. "That was all a dream, Miriam. You dreamed all of it."

Miriam.

My body and blood froze as I reached the halfway point to the tiny kitchen. My body trembled as I turned my head to my right. The living room was over there with its second and third-hand couch and chair. They were empty. The TV was off. I tiptoed over to the counter that separated the kitchen from the entrance and grabbed a vase. The hall lay beyond the kitchen. I leaned to my right and looked down the short corridor.

Nothing. No evil shadows, no creepy guy standing at the end smiling at me. The bathroom and bedroom doors were both open, per my habit. I crept down the hall and peeked into both rooms. Again nothing. I breathed a sigh of relief, but my mind wasn't completely relieves.

I set the vase back on the counter and went about locking my apartment. Sweat soaked my body, so I opted for a very private shower. I grabbed my clothes and slipped into the small, narrow bathroom, but I felt uneasy about turning the shower head on. The noise would obscure the sound of an intruder.

The bathroom door didn't have a lock, but I had a plan. I tucked a spare cloth under the door and a heavy can of hair spray on top of a corner. A little tug and the hair spray toppled over, clattering to the ground with a heavy bang. I returned the can to its corner and stepped back to admire my work. Now nobody could get in without setting off my burglar alarm.

I slipped into the shower and relaxed beneath a waterfall of warmth. The hot water soothed my fears and doubts, and I emerged not only clean but calm. Unfortunately, the calm was only that which comes before a storm as I stepped up to the sink.

Miriam.

DREAMS OF DRAGONS

I shrieked and spun around. The door was shut. There was no one else in the bathroom. I checked the window. Locked. The door was still tightly secured with my burglar alarm still tucked under the entrance. The hair spray stood as an obedient soldier still keeping watch.

My breathing was a little erratic as I turned back to the sink. The mirror was obscured by the steam. I raised my town and wiped the moisture off the mirror. An unfamiliar reflection in the glass made me pause.

A man's face stared at me. A man with red eyes. I screamed and stumbled back into the wall beside the shower. Those red eyes followed me without blinking. I pressed my back and the palms of my hands against the wall as that voice called to me again.

Miriam.

That voice. I dared look at the face in the mirror. The man was about thirty-five with a noon shadow on his pale face. He wore a handkerchief around his head that kept back smooth, short black hair.

"Nimeni."

The voice that spoke was mine. The name passed through my lips unbidden, but I knew what I was saying. I *knew* this face. I stumbled over to the sink and grasped the edges as I looked into the mirror.

"Nimeni?" I repeated. The face smiled and bowed his head, just like the first time I met him. I shook my head. "B-but it can't be. I dreamed it all up." I snort escaped my lips as I recalled exactly what Nimeni was. It was probably the first and only time in history a vampire was his own reflection. "I must still be dreaming." His smile faded and he shook his head. I leaned in closer. "What's wrong? Why don't you say something?"

He reached up and pressed his pale palm against the glass. I started back and my eyes flickered from the hand to the face. "You. . .you want me to touch it?" He nodded. "But why? And why are you here?" My heart quickened as I thought of the others. "Where's Xander? And Darda? And everyone else?" He continued to stare at me with his hand awaiting mine.

I swallowed the lump in my throat and reached up a shaking hand. Our palms touched and I felt a pressure around me. I gasped and shut my eyes.

When I opened them the world had changed.

DREAMS OF DRAGONS

CHAPTER 22

I blinked up at a canopy that surrounded a bed. Billowing curtains surrounded the four familiar posts. I knew this place. I was in my bed at the castle of Alexandria.

I glanced at my right. The other side of the bed had been slept in, but it was now empty. Xander. Darda. Everyone. What had happened?

I jumped out of bed and rushed to the door. The entrance opened before I reached it and Darda stood in the doorway. She held a breakfast tray in her hands. At my close proximity she started back and rattled the dishes on the tray.

"My Lady! What are you doing out of bed so early?"

I grabbed her shoulders and searched her face for answers. "Where's Xander? How did we get here? What happened to Moneta?"

She blinked at me. "Xander is out hunting with Captain Spiros, and we are here at the castle because that is where we reside."

"And Moneta? What happened to her?" I persisted.

She shook her head. "I cannot recall that name."

My mouth dropped open. "How could you forget her? She's trying to kill us!"

Darda furrowed her brow and gave me equal scrutiny. "Kill us? No one is trying to kill us."

"But we were just at her house!" I frowned and turned my face away. "I mean, I was just at my apartment, and then I was here."

Darda leaned in close to me and caught my gaze. "Are you feeling well, Miriam? I could call Apuleius to attend to you.

I dropped my arms and ran a hand through my hair as I half-turned away from her. My eyes lay on the floor, but my thoughts were a fluttering mess. "What the heck is going on here?"

Darda swept past me to the bed and set the tray on the foot of the bed. "Perhaps you had a nightmare. A little bit of food will wipe away those bad thoughts."

I followed her and set a hand on her shoulder. "Darda, tell me the truth. Did we defeat the gods?"

She turned and lay her own hand atop mine. A smile graced her lips that calmed my frayed nerves. "Of course. Don't you remember the final fight with Crates?" I shook my head. Her smile slipped and worry entered her eyes. "Are you sure you are well?"

I nodded. "Yeah, but could you just tell me how we did it? Defeated Crates?"

"With the chime, of course," she told me. She turned to the tray and plucked a cup full of hot tea from among the plates of rolls. "Xander rang the chime and banished him from this world."

"I didn't ring it?" I asked her.

She turned to me and offered me the cup. Her face was a little crestfallen. "No. The chime would not work for you."

DREAMS OF DRAGONS

"But I was the one who could read the inscription," I insisted.

Darda nodded. "You were, but we learned that was merely a ploy by Crates to fool us into your using the chime rather than Xander."

I stared at the ground and ran my hand through my hair. "I couldn't do it?"

Darda set a hand on my shoulder as she grasped the tea saucer in her other one. "To be a failure is nothing to be ashamed about," she consoled me.

That word. That word stirred in me something that felt wrong. *Was* wrong. I whipped my head up and furrowed my brow as I studied her. "What did you say?"

Darda softly smiled at me. "You may be a failure, but we still love you." I looked at the floor and frowned. She tilted her head to one side and studied me with careful eyes. "You truly do not remember any of this, do you?"

I pursed my lips and shook my head. "Not a thing."

Darda pressed the cup of tea against my chest so that I was forced to take it. "Perhaps you are merely tired. Drink this and I will call for Xander-" she turned away toward the door, but I grabbed her arm.

Darda started back and bumped into the tea cup. The cup fell from my hand and shattered on the hard floor.

"What's going on? Who are you?" I questioned her.

"Who am I, Miriam? You know who I am," she insisted as she tried to break free of my hold.

Miriam!

I froze and my eyes widened. Darda took the opportunity to free herself of my grasp and stumble back. She clutched the arm I had grasped and frowned at me. "What is the matter with you, Miriam?" she scolded me.

Miriam! That voice.

I took a step forward and swept my eyes over the room. "Nimeni? Where are you?"

Darda shook her head. "Nimeni is not here, Miriam. There is only you and me."

"Nimeni!" I shouted.

A flicker of movement caught my attention. The vanity had a large mirror on its top that reflected the room. There was one more figure in the mirror than there should have been, one with a pale face.

"Nimeni!" I yelled as I rushed over to the vanity. I set my palms on the top and leaned over. "What the hell happened? Why am I still in this-this-" I waved my hand at the room, "-this dream place?" His expression was tense as he pressed his palm against the other side of the glass. I shook my head. "That didn't work last time. There's got to be something else-"

"Miriam!" Darda yelled as he came up behind me. She grasped my arms and spun me around so that we faced each other. Her expression was a contorted mixture of concern and anger. I'd never seen that combination, and I didn't like it. "Miriam, you must remain in this room-" she guided me roughly over to the bed and pushed me down onto the sheets, "-while I find Xander."

I jumped to my feet and slid out from beside her. She turned to me, but I stepped back and glared at her. "You're not Darda, and this isn't Alexandria, so-" Darda lunged at me and wrapped her arms around me in a tight hug.

Unfortunately for her, she left my hands free. My dragons slipped out and wrapped around *her*. They tore her off of me and raised her off the floor. I side-stepped the floating, thrashing Darda and nodded at the door. "Get her out of here, boys."

"Miriam! Miriam, listen to me!" Darda pleaded as my little dragons flew over to the door with their prisoner. One of them opened the entrance, and with a great toss threw her out into the hall. They slammed the door and locked it by twisting the door handles together.

DREAMS OF DRAGONS

I returned my attention to the mirror and my patient friend. Nimeni still had his hand pressed against the mirror. As our eyes met he pressed his hand tighter on the mirror. I frowned and shook my head. "No, we're going to try something different."

I strode over to the vanity and stood before him. I raised my hand, but I kept my palm a foot away from the glass. My water dragon flowed over my arm and touched his hand. The mirror rippled like water and my serpent slipped through to wrap itself around Nimeni's fingers. Nimeni allowed the serpent to draw him through. I stepped back and watched him slip into the room.

Nimeni stood on both feet and bowed his head to me. "A wonderful idea, My Lady. I feared my way would take you away from me again."

I furrowed my brow. "Take me away how? What is this place?"

Nimeni swept his red eyes over the area and frowned. "This is a memory, and you are captured inside its wonderful throes."

"So it's not a dream?" I mused as I slipped up beside him. I pressed my hand over the top of the vanity before I looked up at the vampire. "Then this is my memory, isn't it?"

He nodded. "Yes. Moneta is using your memories to keep you captive."

I furrowed my brow and shook my head. "But if these are my memories than how are you here?"

He stretched out his hand and brushed the tips of his fingers against my wrist. The healed marks were still visible on my flesh. "Our connection grants me certain powers." His eyes flickered up to mine. "Powers that will diminish in time."

I snorted. "If you think I'm going to start complaining about this right now than you're nuts. Anyway, how do I get out of here and back to waking land?"

He held out his hand to me. "I will guide you there."

I slipped my hand into his and the world around us warped. The walls stretched and the floor became distorted like a swirling puddle of a thousand colors. The ceiling shifted into a dark mist that slowly descended up on like a cloak. I stepped close to the vampire as all became shadows, and all was silence.

"Where are we?" I whispered. I winced when my voice echoed in the darkness.

"The world of my people," he told me. He stepped forward and guided me. "Let me show you the way."

Together we walked into the darkness. After a few steps I felt a deep cold. I paused and wrapped my free arm around myself to stop a shudder. "What's that cold feeling?"

Nimeni looked over his shoulder at me. "The world of the living, but come."

He pulled me along, and the further we walked the colder I became until my legs, shaking from the chill, collapsed beneath me. I fell to my knees, but I didn't lose my connection to my guide. Nimeni knelt beside me. His touch, though cold, was warmer than what I felt.

"We are nearly there," he encouraged me as he wrapped both hands around my own. "Only a few more steps."

A gasp escaped my lips as the cold sank into my very soul. "I-I can't."

He leaned in closer. "You must. For Xander."

Xander. *My* Xander. That goddess might have gotten a hold of him, too. Heck, maybe he's trapped in his memories just like I was, but Nimeni couldn't get him out.

But *I* could.

DREAMS OF DRAGONS

I clenched my teeth and rose. Nimeni guided me through the darkness. One step. Two. My foot reached out for the invisible ground, and suddenly I lost even that much as I stepped into nothing. I fell forward into the darkness. My hand slipped out of Nimeni's own, but his words followed me.

"Good luck, Miriam."

CHAPTER 23

I fell for what felt like eternity, and at the end of forever was a hard splash. Water filled my mouth and clogged my lungs. My fae senses told me which way was up, and I kicked in that direction. A few feet and I burst through the surface. Moldy air never smelled so good.

I was back in that pit full of water. The dim light of freedom hovered a few yards above me. The soggy backpack on my back weighed heavy sloshed against my back, reminding me of the danger and my mission. A shadow above me caught my attention. I tilted my head back and found myself staring into the angry eyes of the goddess of memories, Moneta.

"How could you escape your memories so quickly?" she hissed.

I grinned. "Let's just say I had a guardian angel watching over me."

DREAMS OF DRAGONS

I heard a pounding come from the room above me. Moneta whipped her head up and glared in the direction of the entrance.

"Miriam!" came Xander's muffled voice.

"Xander!" I shouted back, my voice echoing up and down the stone shaft.

Moneta returned her attention to me and a sly smile slipped onto her lips. "Your dragon lord is very persistent. However-" she stood, and I noticed that the opening slowly began to close in from two sides, blotting out the light of hope. "-rest there forever, little fae, and may you remain just a memory to your friends."

She leaned back her head and loosed a laugh that made my blood run cold. Fortunately, it also made it boil. I wasn't going to let this mistress of memory get the better of me, not when she had reminded me that I had so much going for me. Xander, Darda, Spiros and the others. They hadn't given up, and I sure as hell wouldn't be the first to throw in the towel.

I took a deep breath and threw up my arms. My mind was touched by the ocean's endless stories, but I gritted my teeth and focused on the story above me. *My* story. Columns of water rose up around me and slammed into the two stone parts of the closing lid. The water shattered the stone, causing them to rain down on me. One of my columns bent and covered me like a steel bar so that the heavy rocks fell harmlessly into the water.

The water level rose, and I with it. Moneta's eyes widened before her face disappeared from above me. With the way clear I forced the water upward in a rush, and I burst from the opening. I used the water like a slide and slid onto my feet to the floor. Moneta stood behind her throne as my friends burst in through the door. Tucked under one of her arms was the chime.

Xander and Darda were first followed by Spiros and Tillit. Magnus and Alice brought up the rear, and behind them they dragged a mess of sailors from both crews. The foes clashed swords on the stairs and in the hall, and the sound of their shouts and snarls was nearly deafening. The captains slammed the door shut behind the group and barricaded the entrance with the nearby floor candelabras, rugs, and the rotting remains of the wall.

Xander and Darda rushed over to me. He grasped my hands and looked me over. "Are you all right?"

I grinned and nodded. "Yeah, thanks to Nimeni, but Moneta has the chime."

He furrowed his brow. "Nimeni?"

I shook my head. "It's a long story, but we've got bigger fish to fry." I turned around in time to see Moneta pull back the hand on the arm of her chair.

The wall behind the throne drew back and revealed a secret passage. She fled into the darkened space. We rushed over to the opening, and I leaned in. The passage was only three feet wide and led ten feet into the house before it reached a fork where it split into three paths.

Spiros came up to us and looked at Xander. "Should we follow her?"

I had a sinking feeling. "It's got to be a trap," I guessed.

Xander nodded. "I have no doubt because she knows this house better than anyone, but we must follow her."

"And if we catch her and cannot use the chime ourselves?" Spiros asked him.

Xander raised his sword so he grasped it even with his chest. "Then do what you must until we find you."

Magnus set his eyes on the passage that led to the left and nodded at the opening. "Alice and Ah will take that one."

Tillit glanced at Spiros and jerked his head toward the right-hand passage. "Shall we?"

Spiros smiled and bowed his head. "After you."

Our friends hurried down their paths, leaving me with Xander and Darda. Our feet clattered along the old floorboards, startling clouds of dust from their long slumber. I used my water to douse the dry dirt at the same time that we raced left and right around sharp corners.

The darkness became nearly impenetrable to my weak eyes until I finally stumbled over a loose board. I fell forward and grabbed at anything. My hands caught on a shelf that jutted out from the wall and kept me from slamming into the hard plank floor.

"How big is this house?" I snapped.

Xander squinted into the gloom ahead of us and pursed his lips. "I believe we are nearly at the end." I followed his gaze and noticed a faint glow around the next corner.

"How are we to retrieve the chime?" Darda whispered.

"In whatever way is necessary," Xander advised her.

We crept forward and peeked around the corner. The corridor ended at a narrow, winding staircase that led into the ceiling. A single floor candelabra stood at the base of the steps as though beckoning us.

"I'm liking this less and less," I whispered.

"What choice do we have?" Xander pointed out.

We continued to the steps and paused. Xander tested the first step. The stairs groaned under his weight. He tilted his head back and looked up the winding stairs. The steps wound around a large post through the ceiling and up six floors to a landing. A thin railing provided support, otherwise a traveler was liable to fall into the narrow gap between the steps and the wall.

"Can we fly?" Darda asked him.

He shook his head. "The stairwell is too narrow." He turned to me and held out his hand. "I can carry you."

I snorted. "I might not be that fat after all these months of being in this world, but I'm not about to combine our weight on any of those steps."

"Then give me your hand."

"Now *that* I'll do."

Xander held my hand and we eased up the creaking old stairs. Some of them were broken in half and gave us a view through their cracks to the hard floor below. The higher we climbed the more shaky the support post became so that soon the whole structure began to sway to and fro.

We were halfway up the stairs when a resounding crack came from the post. My two companions and I froze. I looked up at Xander who stood on the next step with his foot gently on the one above that.

"Please tell me that was you," I pleaded.

He shook his head. "It was not."

The structure beneath us groaned. I heard a board break and felt the railing lean away from me as one of its braces gave way. Xander wrapped his arms around me and Darda slipped between me and oblivion. She braced herself on what remained of the once-firm railing and held me back.

The sudden movements of my valorous friends destabilized the center post. A crack appeared on the surface of the wood and ran up and down its length. Little splinters appeared, hairline fractures that spelled inevitable doom. A point in the post five feet above us leaned rightward, taking with it the mess of wood it held up.

"Jump!" Xander yelled.

He pushed Darda and me off the stairs as the whole structure collapsed on our heads. We were shoved against the curved wall and fell toward the floor. Darda clutched onto me with her on the bottom. Xander opened his wings and protected us from the falling stakes and shards of broken wood as the staircase destroyed itself.

It was a race against us and the crashing wood that followed us down. Unfortunately, we were the winners as we reached the floor a half second before the structure. The boards clattered on top of Xander and part of the broken beam slammed into the wall above our heads. It locked into place at an angle over us as though trying to protect us from itself. Dust flew up, choking and blinding us.

The whole episode lasted only fifteen seconds, but it felt like an eternity. Than the crash ended and all was quiet. The dust cleared and Xander sat up. He winced as a ton of debris slid off his back and onto the floor behind him.

His eyes fell on me and he looked over my sore form. "Are you all right?"

I sat up and allowed an inch of dust to slide off me. "I think so."

A groan from beneath me made me move aside and look at where I had lain. Darda lay with her back on the floor. Her face was pale and one of her legs was at an odd angle.

My eyes widened as my gaze fell on her odd limb. "Darda! I'm so sorry!"

She smiled, though the gesture was a little shaky. "There is no need to apologize. My ample form cushioned the fall."

"Can you stand?" Xander asked her.

"I am fine," Darda assured us. She tried to stand, but her face contorted with pain and she fell back to the floor.

"Hold still," Xander instructed her as he studied her leg. He pursed his lips and his eyes flickered up to her face. "Your leg is broken."

Darda raised her chin and stiffened her jaw. "I will not allow that to stop me," she insisted as she tried to stand.

I pushed her back to the floor. "But we will. You stay here and Xander and I will be the heroes."

I made to stand, but Darda grasped my wrist. Her eyes met mine, and in their depths was fear mixed with pride. "Be safe, and give that terrible goddess a good slap for me."

I grinned and nodded. "Sure thing."

Xander and I stood, and I tilted my head back to take in the view above us. The top half of the stairs were gone, and the bottom half was wrecked. Only a few odd steps remained.

I glanced up at Xander who stood by my side. "So how do we get up there to be the heroes?"

He tucked his wings against his back and crouched down. "Climb onto my back and I will climb the wall."

I grinned. "Don't mind if I do."

I climbed onto his back and wrapped my arms around his neck. Xander pinned me against him with his folded wings, and with my knees tucked tightly against his back he strode over to the wall. That was mostly intact, minus the damage done by time that Moneta no longer bothered to hide. Xander's hands stretched into claws, and he slammed them into the wall above his head. The wood broke under his hands, but gave him a good hold. Thus began our climb.

That was the running mantra in my mind as I squished myself against Xander's back and tried not to look down. That worked for the first ten feet, and then I dared a peek over my shoulder. Yep, it was a long, hard drop to a floor that was littered with sharp, stabbing debris. A single slip would mean a worse injury than what happened to Darda.

I shut my eyes and turned my face away. The things we did to be heroes.

DREAMS OF DRAGONS

CHAPTER 24

After a few tense minutes Xander reached the top. The landing still existed so that he sidled up to the floor and climbed aboard. I rolled off of him and would have kissed the ground it if hadn't been covered in the dust from the collapse.

I stood and looked at the way before us. A straight corridor some fifty feet long finished at a wood door. Planks covered the walls and floor, and their age was showing. Worms had eaten away at the wood, leaving large holes that I could fit my hand through. Mold aspired to control the rest of the surface as it grew in large patches on the ceiling and walls.

Our path had brought us closer to the roof, and to the noise of the storm outside. The winds battered at the roof and gave a little vibration to the floor. The wood groaned under the strain, and I saw some of the boards bend beneath such power.

"This place just keeps getting nicer and nicer," I mused.

"That may be to our advantage," Xander suggested.

I frowned and looked up at him. "Dying of mold is to our advantage?"

"The condition of the house may be a reflection of Moneta's inability to control her powers. That implies that she is afraid, and in such a state she will be easier to handle," he pointed out.

I sighed and looked back down the corridor. "*If* we can manage her at all, especially since she has the chime."

"I will retrieve the chime from her and you must use it," he advised me.

I pursed my lips and stared hard at the floor. "But what if Crates lied about that, too?" My eyes flickered up to Xander's tense face. His silence uneased me. "What if I'm not the one who's supposed to ring the bell? What if it doesn't work at all?"

He clasped my hands in his and smiled down at me. "I have no doubt you will be able to use the chime. Not only because you are my Maiden but because you are a gift to this world, a gift that will save it."

A blush brightened my cheeks, but I squeezed his hands. "How about after this we take a vacation? A real one, and maybe one that'd last longer than a day."

He nodded. "I would like that very much."

The tender moment was ruined by a nearly inaudible shuffling noise. We both stiffened and swept our eyes around the area.

I stabbed a finger at a nearby wall. "There!"

There was a squeak of rusted hinges and a panel opened on our right. Xander and I leapt back and tensed as we prepared for a fight. What we got was a piggish snout followed by the familiar figure of Tillit. He slipped out of the hole and shut the opening behind him.

Xander frowned. "Where is Spiros?"

DREAMS OF DRAGONS

Tillit jerked his head over his shoulder. "Back there somewhere. The passage split into two and he went one way and I went the other." He looked among our group and his eyes widened. "Where's Darda?"

"Injured, but otherwise fine. A staircase collapsed," Xander assured our concerned friend.

Tillit wrinkled his nose. "That explains the noise I heard, but she's okay, right?"

"Well, but waiting for us to finish our mission," Xander reminded him.

Another creaking noise caught my attention. I looked past the others at the long hall. The door, once shut, slowly creaked open a few inches.

"Uh, guys," I spoke up as I pointed at the entrance that was ajar. "I think she's getting impatient."

Tillit hiked up his pants and grinned. "Then we'd better not keep her waiting."

"Shouldn't we wait for the others?" I suggested.

A loud boom over our heads heralded the worsening of the storm. The wind picked up

We all jerked our heads back and watched as the boards on the ceiling rattled. I yelped and leapt into the middle of the hall when the clapboard walls already began to shudder. Nails were pried loose and dropped to the floor like hard drops of rain.

"Look out!" Xander shouted as he grabbed my shoulders and pulled me deeper into the corridor.

Tillit followed us and narrowly avoided a terrible end when the walls and ceiling collapsed, shutting off the landing to us. A cloud of dust blasted us so that Tillit waved his hand in front of his face and wrinkled his nose.

"I don't-*cough*-think she wants us to wait," Tillit guessed.

Xander pursed his lips and half-turned to the door. "Then we must go."

The storm continued its fury as we walked down the hall, but the walls and ceiling remained in place. We reached the door and Xander swung it open, revealing the interior to all of us. Beyond the door was a large, hexagonal room. The open ceiling revealed the large beams that supported the peaked roof. The walls were of clapboard, as was the floor, and along each flat wall was a tall, wide mirror totaling six. The mirrors reflected our pale faces as the storm raged above us.

At the back of the room was a high-backed chair made of bones. The arms were arm bones and the legs were made of leg bones. The back was likewise made out of its namesake material, and atop the back was a row of grinning skulls.

Moneta sat atop those bones-her victims-and smiled at us. In her lap was the Theos Chime. She stretched out her hands on either side of her and used them to gesture about the room. "Welcome to my last refuge."

We slipped into the room and Xander stepped up in front of Tillit and me. "What do you hope to gain by delaying your sending?"

Moneta laughed and lay a hand over the top of the chime. "Delaying? Dragon lord, I intend to destroy your one and only hope in sending me." Tillit snorted. Moneta's amusement slipped a little as she looked past Xander to frown at the sus. "That is an annoying sound."

He shrugged. "I couldn't help it. That was pretty funny."

She narrowed her eyes. "How so?"

He nodded at the chime. "If you could destroy that thing than you would've done it already."

A sly smile slipped onto her lips as she tilted her head to one side and stroked the chime. "How very observant of you, but are you observant enough to notice where you are?"

I frowned and looked over the room. The mirrors reflected my face, but something more. The walls at my back trembled. Their nails shook and vibrated out of their holes, but the holes didn't remain empty for long. I gasped as blood flowed out of the holes and onto the floor. The life liquid splashed across the boards and slid up to me like a tide coming in.

I yelped and jumped back, but the blood was too fast. It covered my feet in a few seconds and showed no signs of slowing as the blood climbed my pants.

"Miriam!" Xander shouted as he reached out to me.

His hand was inches from me when one of the walls burst, sending a torrential flood of blood into the room. The flow swept me off my feet and slammed me against a nearby wall. I was pinned in place and could only watch as Xander and Tillit struggled to move in the thick juice.

Moneta continued to sit on her throne, a sick smile on her face as the blood reached her chin. She winked at me before the blood swallowed her whole. Another wall burst, sending in another horrendous wave of blood. I tilted my head back and shut my eyes against the terrible flood as the blood lapped at my neck.

Not like this! I thought to myself. *Not when we're so close!*

Then something stung my cheek and jerked my head to one side. I stumbled forward and opened my eyes. The room was as it should have been. No blood, no broken walls. Only my friends and the goddess. Xander stood beside me cradling a red cheek in his hand and glaring at Moneta.

Her face was contorted with anger as she leapt to her feet. Her dark eyes looked past me. "*You.*"

I spun around. Tillit stood behind me with one hand cradled in the other. "Your magic's not bad, but my nose is better. I could smell your spell from a mile away."

I glared at my former friend. "You hit me, didn't you?"

He sheepishly grinned at me. "It worked, didn't it?"

"We must stay focused," Xander reminded us as our foe stood.

Moneta held the chime in her palm and raised the bell above her head. "Such fools. You believe I will allow you to send me with this pathetic bell?"

Xander took a step toward her. "I doubt the chime can be so easily broken by smashing it to the floor."

"Now just be a good goddess and let us ring it so you can go home," Tillit spoke up.

Moneta closed her eyes and leaned her head back. A bitter smile slipped onto her lips. "What you do to me can never be as cruel as what time has done. What *he* has done."

"He only wanted to protect his library," I argued.

Her eyes flung open and she sneered at me. "His *precious* library, but what about me? I offered him my love and he gave me *nothing!*"

The storm that raged outside turned for the worst. The walls and ceilings rattled with its intensity as the wind tried to break its way inside. The mirrors dropped off the walls and shattered into a million small pieces, each rendering a little different picture of the room.

Moneta's reflection showed her in a million different ways. She was my father, Xander's mother, her old-woman self. Even Crates was represented.

Moneta looked down at the image of the god and her face softened. She lowered her arm a little and shook her head. "My love. Why could you not love me back?"

DREAMS OF DRAGONS

Xander leapt at her and tried to snatch the chime from her hand. Moneta leapt back out of his reach and clutched the chime in both hands in front of her. Her soft expression hardened and the storm outside worsened. The wall boards rattled and some clattered to the floor, revealing a thin wall that lay between us and the merciless winds. Rain soaked the boards and slipped in through the cracks, creating puddles that crept toward us.

Moneta raised the chime in both her hands above her head and glared at us. "You will not have this chime!"

CHAPTER 25

Thunder struck the house and immediately I smelled smoke. My eyes widened as I understood its meaning. "The house is on fire!"

My last word was drowned out by the roar of the wind. The gale tore away at the flimsy exterior siding and pulled apart whole walls. Xander and Tillit pressed against me on either side as the wind tried to throw us off the roof. The barren island was revealed to us, along with a ghastly sight.

The crew of the Acheron floated around us, their bodies aglow with an unnatural light. They surrounded the small room in which we stood, and their lifeless eyes stared accusingly at us. The rain pelted us like tiny whips, but the water went right through those long-dead memories.

The thunderous booms shook the air as Moneta stretched her arms higher as lightning flashed across the black sky. One of the spears of light slammed into the chime in

DREAMS OF DRAGONS

her hands, creating a horrible gong-like sound that made me wince.

"She's trying to destroy it!" Tillit shouted above the wind.

Not on my watch. I whipped out my hand and a thick water dragon emerged. It fought against the stormy wind to slip around the body of the chime. With a quick yank the bell was pulled from her grasp and my dragon returned to me. I grabbed the chime and clutched it to my chest. The metal was hot to the touch, courtesy of the lightning strike, but was otherwise unharmed.

"Use it!" Tillit snapped.

I clutched the bell between my hands in front of me and rung it. The chime echoed over the ruins of the manor house. Moneta clapped her hands over her ears and loosed a terrible, high-pitched scream. The sending started at the bottom as her feet began to disappear. Another ring and the transparency climbed higher.

She wasn't the only one affected. The sailors, their captain among them, clutched their hands over their ears and opened their mouths in terrible screams. Their horrible cries of pain rang nearly as loudly as my bell as they twisted and scratched at their ears until they bled. They didn't have the luxury of the kneeling position for long as their lower halves, too, vanished until they lay weak on the ground.

I raised the bell for a last ring, but a voice stopped me.

"Wait!" Abraxas gasped as he floated closer to me. His eyes showed awareness as he stretched out one hand at me. "Please do not exile her! My men cannot survive without her!"

Xander stepped up beside me and shook his head. "Your men died long ago, captain."

Abraxas's eyes fell on me as he clenched one hand into a fist before him. "Mercy! Mercy for my men!"

I raised the bell for the death knell of many. Moneta rallied and threw up one arm to the dark sky. Another flash of lightning illuminate the sky and struck the chime. Even in the storm I heard a faint crinkling sound sheets of wrapping paper rubbing together. I yelped and leapt back, dropping the bell. It clattered to the floor and rolled toward the edge.

"The chime!" I yelled.

Tillit scrambled for the chime and caught the chime before it flew over into the oblivion. He scurried back to me and clasped it tight in my hands. The heavy sus was winded and his face pale. "Don't make me do that again."

I grasped the handle with both hands and smiled. My joy was short-lived when we heard a din of laughter. The sound came from the crew and their mistress as Moneta led the group in the strange sound.

The goddess held out her hand to me and grinned from ear to ear. "Go ahead and ring my doom! Ring it!"

"Wait!" Tillit shouted as he lunged forward and grabbed my wrist. He pointed at a small spot on the bell in my hand. "There's something wrong with it!"

I squinted my eyes and beheld a nearly invisible hairline crack along the height of the bell. It ran from beneath the handle to the lip of the mouth. A single gong of the clapper would reverberate the bell and lead to something bad happening.

I turned to Tillit and blinked at him. "How did you see that?"

He dropped his hold of me and grinned. "What's a good trader for?"

Xander looked from the bell to our foe and glared at her. "What have you done to the chime?"

Moneta stood straight and tall. "I have instilled within the chime a memory-*my* memory-of all those long years I have waited in this house for him to come to me. That-" her eyes fell on the crack. A wild look slipped into their depths and a sly, wide smile appeared on her lips. "That is the power of my grief. That tiny crack may appear pathetic, but to harm the chime requires a great deal of strength." A long, low chuckle escaped her lips. The sound turned my blood cold. "Now Crates and I will be together forever in this world, and I will be loosed upon it with all the wrath that my heart desires." She floated over to one of the tall broken windows and smiled out upon the weakening storm. "If Crates refuses to love me and he refuses to leave then I shall destroy the world he loves so much."

Xander whipped his head to Tillit. "Are you able to repair the damage?"

Tillit pursed his lips and shook his head. "Not this. Even if I knew how to fix a bell I think this one's a little to special for a simple patch."

"What of your bag?"

"I doubt it."

"You must look!"

As the men went back and forth I wracked my mind for ideas. There had to be a way to fix the chime. It was made before, it could be fixed!

In the midst of that storm, surrounded by ghosts and hopelessness, a memory came to me. It was of Crates before we began this long adventure.

You will tested the worst of all, Miriam, so I will give you further advice: keep the chime to yourself and do not give it over to anyone.

I looked down at the chime that lay in my palms, so fragile now. It was hope made solid, and I had to be the one to be its ringer, but how? How did I stand apart from my companions?

One of the many raindrops fell onto my hands and pooled in my palm beneath the chime. At the touch the bell sparkled for a moment, but the light faded when the raindrop slipped through the crack between my hands and dropped to the ground.

My eyes widened. That was it. That's how I could do it. I clasped the chime handle in both hands and focused on the upraised bell.

Moneta sneered at me. "You dare to try? The bell will not finish its ring before it shatters forever."

Water flowed from my hands and encapsulated the metal hood with a thin layer of my power. The clapper pressed against my water without touching the metal.

Moneta, her body hardly more than a shadow, took a step back, but her expression was still one of defiance. "Your pathetic power cannot save the bell."

I raised the bell and grinned at her. "Wanna bet?"

Her eyes widened as I brought the bell down. She lunged at me and stretched out her hand to grab the chime, but the clapper slammed into the inner walls of the bell, sounding her death knell.

A single, clear ring came from the chime and echoed across the rooftops. Moneta screamed and her ghostly crew vanished like puffs of smoke.

A bolt of lightning crashed down from the sky and struck the platform. I felt a sharp pain in my body as the electricity raced up my legs. The world turned black and I lost consciousness.

CHAPTER 26

I expected a lot of pain when I woke up-if I woke up-but what I got was a lot of dizziness. Even with my eyes shut the world spun around me. Something soft-like a down pillow-brushed against my face. The sensation tickled me and brought a shaky smile to my lips. The mystery something did it again. I drew away and my eyes fluttered open.

What I saw were rows and rows of books, and the endless floors that stretched up to the glass ceiling. The Mallus Library. I lay on the floor of its prime story, and a large shadow stood over me. The shadow had glimmering yellow eyes. I yelped and sat up.

"You are frightening her, Justum," Crates' voice called out.

The griffin hung its head and took a few steps back. There was a groan, but it didn't come from me. I sat up and looked around myself. Xander and Tillit lay on the ground close beside me. It was Tillit who announced to the world he was waking up, and not in the best of health.

He sat up and clutched his head. "That was not enjoyable."

I scrambled over to Xander. He lay on his face with his arms bent above his head. I rolled him onto his back and looked him over. His breathing was fine and I didn't see any wounds.

I grasped one of his hands in mine. "Xander?" His eyes flickered open. A smile slipped onto my lips, and that held back the tears in my eyes. "About time."

He swept his gaze over where he lay. "Where-?"

I followed his searching eyes and pursed my lips. "I think we're in the Mallus Library."

"You are," Crates' voice spoke up. The master of the library stepped out from around the corner and stopped a few yards short of us. His hands were clasped behind him and he looked softly at our little ragged group. The griffin walked up to his side and both turned to face us.

I helped Xander to his feet and shook his head. "But how'd we get here?"

Tillit climbed to his feet and nodded. "Yeah, I don't remember walking through a door." He winced and rubbed his head. "Maybe *into* a door."

"You traveled through the door that connects the world of the living to that of the dead," Crates revealed. "It is Moneta's final revenge upon you for sending her to our world."

My mouth dropped open. "You. . .you mean we're dead?"

"You are between worlds, or rather, in *my* world where time is suspended," he explained.

"Then we will die if we leave here, as the library will disappear if removed from your influence," Xander guessed.

Crates smiled and shook his head. "No. I learned from my error and removed all of you from your time a

DREAMS OF DRAGONS

moment before the worst was to happen." He raised his hand and gestured to a point beyond us. We all turned to see the door that stood at the end of the wide hall. "You are free to leave and return to the land of the living when your last deed is done."

I returned my attention to him and frowned. "And what's that?"

He stood straight, but there was sorrow in the lines of his face. "The bell must be rung one more time."

My mouth dropped open. "But if I ring it then you'll-"

He held out his hands in front of him. In his cupped palms was the charred remains of the chime. The wooden handle was a blackened mess, and the bell itself was twisted nearly beyond recognition. "Then I will disappear, and this world will be safe."

Tillit pointed at the bell. "I'd hate to tell you, but that isn't going to be ringing anytime soon."

Crates smiled and a light appeared from his palms. The light surrounded the bell in a transparent, glowing ball through which we could the bell. A soft mist floated over the bell and soaked into the charred remains. My eyes widened as I watched the metal un-corrode and reform itself into its perfect shape. A handle sprouted from the top, as good as new. Time had been reversed by the god of time.

Xander pursed his lips as he looked from the bell to Crates' face. "Need we send you?"

Crates chuckled. "I would never have expected those words from you, Dragon Lord, but yes, I must be sent. This world is yours now, and I will not interfere any longer."

I lifted my head and gazed out over the vast shelves of books. "But what'll happen to the library?"

He lifted his eyes to the majesty of the building and sighed. "Without a librarian the magic is gone, and the library will fall out of its place in time and revert back to when I saved it."

"Then it will be destroyed," Xander surmised.

Crates nodded. "It will."

My face fell. "But all this knowledge-everything you worked for-will be gone."

"It was never meant to be saved by anyone," he pointed out.

I frowned. "But it *was*, and to just let it be destroyed-" I shook my head. "-it'd be like Moneta really did win."

"What if the library still had a librarian?" Tillit spoke up.

Crates glanced at the sus and arched an eyebrow. "What do you mean?"

"Like someone took over after you left. You know, a new librarian," Tillit suggested.

Crates furrowed his brow, but a smile teased the corners of his lips. "An intriguing idea, but I haven't much time to choose a worthy candidate."

Tillit puffed out his chest. "I can take the job. It sounds cushy."

Crates blinked at him. "Do you know how to read?"

Tillit's face fell and his chest deflated. "Who do you think's been reading all this stuff for these two?"

The librarian chuckled. "Pardon my teasing, Master Tillit. I am well aware of your abilities, and know you would be a suitable librarian."

"Then it is possible to transfer the powers of the library without it falling back into its time?" Xander asked our host.

Crates nodded. "I will guarantee it after my passing, though I must warn you that the life of the librarian is very lonely." The griffin took a step forward and squawked. Crates chuckled. "I see. It is true you needn't go with me, but are you sure?" The beast squawked again, and Crates bowed his head. "Then I will leave you to watch over him."

DREAMS OF DRAGONS

Tillit eyed the overgrown turkey with hesitation. "I don't know-" The griffin frowned and squawked at him. He held up his hands. "Okay, okay, you can stay."

Xander turned to his old friend and studied him with sorrowful eyes. "You are sure you wish to remain here?"

Tillit grinned. "Why not? Running around with you two has made me a little tired, and this library would make a good place to rest." I set a hand on his shoulder. He half-turned to me and patted my hand. "Don't you worry about old Tillit. He'll be fine, and if you ever need me I'll be a doorway away."

Crates' eyes fell on me and he held out the fixed bell. "Are you prepared?"

Tillit held up his hand. "There's something I need to do." He turned to me and took my arm before he led me to the side. The sus lowered his voice so the other three wouldn't overhear him. "Do you think you could do Tillit one last favor?"

I sniffled, but gave a nod and a small smile. "Sure thing."

"Could you-that is-" he cleared his throat and I detected a hint of a sniffle, "-could you tell dear Darda that-well, that I'm going to miss the old woman and her badgering me?"

I nodded. "Of course."

"Oh, and this-" he slipped off his satchel and hung it around my neck. I nearly collapsed beneath its weight. "-it's got everything I own, including my autobiography. I don't expect it'll finish any time soon, but I'd like people to be able to read about everything up to here."

I clutched my shaking hands around the strap of the bag and nodded. "I'll make sure everybody reads it, even people who can't read."

He chuckled. "You're something else, Miriam."

"It is time," Crates spoke up.

Tillit released me and I stepped around him. Crates walked up to me and held the bell out. I grasped the handle in one shaking, but paused as my eyes flickered up to his.

"You're sure?" I asked him.

He bowed his head. "Very much so."

I pursed my lips, but accepted the bell and took a step back. I raised the chime in my hand and-with a deep breath-rang the bell. The clapper struck the sides and the soft sound of the ringing echoed up and down the grand library.

Crates smiled as his form began to fade. "Goodbye, my friends. Take good care of your wonderful world."

His form vanished into the air, but as he disappeared a faint light appeared around him. The light formed itself into a ball that hovered in the empty air for a moment before it flitted over to float before Tillit. He stretched his hand out and touched the light with the tip of his pudgy finger. The light slipped into him and ran up his body, illuminating his form in a soft glow.

"Wow. . ." Tillit whispered as he held up his glowing hands.

I dropped my arm to my side and hung my head. Xander came up beside me and laid his hands on my shoulders. I looked up at him. Tears slid down my cheeks. "Did we really do the right thing?"

He nodded. "It is what he wished."

Tillit rubbed his hands together and the light brightened. "All right, let's see about getting you two back home." He looked at the door and waved a hand. The door swung open, and through the portal we could see the deck of Magnus' ship. Tillit turned to us and smiled. "All aboard for the ship back to Alexandria." A stifled sob escaped my lips before I rushed over and gave him a big hug. His face softened and he returned the hug. He leaned his head down beside mine and lowered his voice. "Keep good care of that dragon lord of ours. He's a lot of trouble."

DREAMS OF DRAGONS

I stepped back away from him and even though I couldn't stop crying I gave him a little smile and a nod. "Will do."

Xander came up behind me and bowed his head to Tillit. "We will see each other again."

Tillit grinned and puffed out his chest. "You can count on it, now off you go!"

Xander drew me away and to the door. I paused in front of the threshold and looked over my shoulder. Tillit stood silhouetted against the hundreds of books. At his side stood Justum. He gave a wave.

I smiled and nodded before I turned to look ahead. Together Xander and I walked through the door and back to the living world.

CHAPTER 27

The ship rocked to and fro on the gentle seas as we stepped onto her deck. A slam made me look behind us. The entrance to the captain's quarters was shut. That had been our doorway.

"Miriam!" The shout came from Darda who rushed over to us as quickly as her splint-wrapped leg would allow. She crashed into me and gave me a bone-crushing hug. "I thought I would never see you again!"

Spiros followed her and stopped before Xander. "How did you manage to escape the house?"

"A little help from Crates, but what has happened?" Xander asked him.

Spiros half-turned to the starboard side of the ship. He nodded at the distance. "That."

We followed his gaze. A huge bonfire burned in the distance, and by its silhouette I recognized Moneta's island. It was completely engulfed in flames.

DREAMS OF DRAGONS

The storm around us was gone, and above our heads was a clear blue sky. The sun shone down on us and cast a warm glow on our skin.

Spiros looked back to Xander. "The thunder caught the rotten boards afire. We barely made it out, and have been searching for you for over an hour."

"Crates stole us from Moneta's revenge and had us send him," Xander finished the tale.

Spiros nodded. "Then it is over. The gods are gone."

Darda pulled us apart and looked me over. "You are not-" she froze when her gaze fell on my chest. Her eyes widened when she recognized Tillit's satchel and she whipped her head up to meet my gaze. "Tillit. . .is he-?"

I grasped the strap and shook my head. "No, but he's got a new job."

"That is a miracle unto itself," Spiros quipped.

"He will be managing the Mallus Library from this day forward," Xander revealed.

Spiros folded his arms over his chest and smiled. "I never thought I would have seen the day when he acquired a steady line of work."

Darda stepped up to me and pursed her lips as she studied my face. "Is he. . .is he happy?"

I smiled at her and gave a nod. "Very happy, and he told me to tell you that he's going to miss you badgering him."

There were tears in his eyes as she shook her head. "That old fool."

Magnus walked up to us, and at his sides were Alice and Nimeni. I turned to the vampire and grinned at him. "Thanks for the help back there. I wouldn't have been able to find my way without you."

He smiled and bowed deeply to me. "It was my pleasure, My Lady."

Magnus turned to Xander. "Where to, My Lord?"

Xander smiled. "Home, captain. Home."

"Captain!" a sailor called from the crow's nest. He pointed at the sea ahead of us. Another ship was coming.

Alice breathed a sigh of relief. "About time. I can finally get off this hunk of junk and onto a *clean* ship."

Magnus looped his arm around her waist and grinned at her. "It's been fun, though, hasn't it?"

She rolled her eyes, but a smile teased the corners of her lips. "I suppose."

We sailed home aboard the vessel, our final voyage after many adventures. My thoughts wandered over the places I'd seen and the people I'd met. The good and the bad mingled to create a life I could never have imagined, and one I wouldn't have traded for the world.

A few hours later found Xander and I seated on a crate near the bow of the ship. As the sun set over the wide horizon I leaned my head against his shoulder and admired the beauty of the world. "Did I ever tell you I'm glad to be your Maiden?"

He wrapped an arm around me and drew me against his side. I reveled in the warmth of his body as he looked down at me with a smile. "No, and I would not mind hearing those words for many years."

And for many years he did hear it as we enjoyed the coming retirement from adventure. There would be troubles and tribulations, but life was like that and I wouldn't have had it any other way.

A note from Mac

Thank you for purchasing my book! Your support means a lot to me, and I'm grateful to have the opportunity to entertain you with my stories.

If you'd like to continue reading the series, or wonder what else I might have up my writer's sleeve, feel free to check out my website at *macflynn.com*, or contact me at mac@macflynn.com.

* * *

Want to get an email when the next book is released? Sign up for the Wolf Den, the online newsletter with a bite, at *eepurl.com/tm-vn*!

Other series by Mac Flynn

Contemporary Romance
Being Me
Billionaire Seeking Bride
The Family Business
Loving Places
PALE Series
Trapped In Temptation

Demon Romance
Ensnare: The Librarian's Lover
Ensnare: The Passenger's Pleasure
Incubus Among Us
Lovers of Legend
Office Duties
Sensual Sweets
Unnatural Lover

Dragon Romance
Blood Dragon
Dragon Bound
Maiden to the Dragon

Ghost Romance
Phantom Touch

Vampire Romance
Blood Thief
Blood Treasure
Vampire Dead-tective
Vampire Soul

Urban Fantasy Romance
Death Touched

Werewolf Romance
Alpha Blood
Alpha Mated
Beast Billionaire
By My Light
Desired By the Wolf
Falling For A Wolf
Garden of the Wolf
Highland Moon
In the Loup
Luna Proxy
Marked By the Wolf
Moon Chosen
The Moon and the Stars
Moon Lovers
Oracle of Spirits
Scent of Scotland: Lord of Moray
Shadow of the Moon
Sweet & Sour
Wolf Lake

Manufactured by Amazon.ca
Bolton, ON